A Time in Nostalgia

By Jessica Garrow
Craig Garrow

A Time in Nostalgia

Copyright : 2015 by Jessica Garrow
Craig Garrow

Cover by: Jessica Garrow
Craig Garrow
Illustrated by:
Jessica Garrow

All rights reserved. No part of this book may be reproduced in any form by any electronic or mechanical means including photocopying, recording, or information storage and retrieval without permission in writing from the author.

ISBN-13: 978-1517616816
ISBN-10: 1517616816

Book Website
www.atimeinnostalgia.com

Give feedback on the book at:
www.facebook.com/atimeinnostalgia

Dedicated to

Effie Christie
Rose Masa
Harold Garrow

And many thanks to our brothers, sisters, friends, and family

Contents

1. The Trip 7
2. Detective Work 17
3. The Shop 27
4. A Ghost and New Friend 37
5. Run Away 47
6. Hard Lesson 65
7. New Clothes 73
8. Some Changes 83
9. The Library 97
10. Past Shadows 107
11. Planet Phoenix 119
12. All Grown Up 131
13. Trill 141

14. Team Work 153

15. Up to Us 169

16. Is Time Travel for Me 179

Tobin

A Time in Nostalgia

Chapter 1

The Trip

It would be the time of day in the afternoon that the sun would shine warmth on your face if you lived on a planet near a sun. For Tobin Guide it was just a boring time cycle with dull lights and panels. Living on a research station for a ten year old boy often puts him in a comatose state making him crave any stimulation that is not control panel or on board computer related. The occasional photo on the corridors walls was not enough color for him. What would it be like on a colony planet, he often thought to himself? He had only seen holo programs of trees, nature, and wild life. The station did not have much in the potted plant garden to speak of.

A calling voice of a man snapped Tobin out of his daze. It was his Uncle Stan Venkman saying "Hey, do you listen to anything around you? The children's monitor group leader just informed me that you'll need supervision tomorrow. They are remodeling the care center and do to the lack of research lately I get to take you with me on my shift." Tobin and Stan exchanged looks. Stan added "Well, I'm sure you won't be too much to handle right?"

If you asked Stan about his nephew, he would say he was a young brown eyed, brunette boy, who was stubborn and bull headed. Stan had thought to himself and was hoping Tobin would just sit and sulk for the day. Tobin's parents would leave him with friends and family quite often actually. While they went to build and set up other stations this caused Tobin to brood a lot, this making him suffer socially. Now he was Stan's to take care of indefinitely. The years have passed and Tobin still treats his uncle as a stranger; keeping himself disconnected from everyone. Not showing any interest in a relationship with his uncle or anyone else.

Stan tapped Tobin on the side while saying "Come on let's go to our quarters to get you fed and to bed; I know I'll need the sleep."

Dinner was bland and boring to Tobin, sitting there picking at his food, he was just going to leave most of it for Stan to throw out. Stan trying to grab Tobin's attention said "Don't think that you'll be getting out of studying, you can consider your homework load to be doubled."

Tobin sighed and pushed his plate away, got up, grabbed his study port, and went to his room and plugged it into his holo stand. Tobin flipped through the study program, not even looking at it. If he wanted he could do the weeks' worth of work in one day. What a bore he thought to himself to learn about things that he would never see in person. An hour passed and his uncle poked his head in to see if he was still studying. Stan stood with a short pause and then walked off to his own room for the night. Tobin quickly opened a game program to keep occupied if you could call it a game. Even the games the youth could use were full of learning problems you had to do to get to play the more fun levels. After a while Tobin turned off his holo port then went and lay on his bed to stare at the ceiling. Tobin thought what would it be like to be really living a life and not this artificial existence, that he was told was a great way to live. They said living in search of new knowledge in this air tight sterile station was the best thing anyone could achieve. There must be something more for me thought Tobin as his eyes closed and there was black for what seemed a little bit of time; morning came fast.

On a lower deck in a research room stood Tobin, he was watching people poke and fiddle with instruments of all kinds. His uncle was across the room talking to a younger woman with black straight hair. She wasn't showing much interest in Stan and was more involved in her work. Not to say Stan wasn't a looker mind you, he had blond hair, beard, and blue eyes. Tobin really doubted how much blood there was between them, after all his uncle was no flirt and lacked much in personality or so Tobin thought. Stan obsessed about his tasks and never took time for fun.

Stan stopped talking to the lady and walked up to Tobin and began to say "Well it seems we are going on a bit of a field trip. Sarah has just informed me the staff is in need of tools and parts."

Tobin responded with "So?"

"The supply ship will not be here for another week." Stan said with a happy tone.

Tobin looked puzzled. Stan added to help him understand "It means we are going to Nostalgia to pick some up."

"What's that?" asked Tobin.

"It's a space station on the other side of Alpha Phoenix's moon." Stan replied with a grin.

"I've never heard of it."

"We don't use it too often as a supplier, our funding does not approve of its business classification. It's not up to their codes."

"Not up to code? Funding? Then why go there?"

"OK, it's like this; we have to pull out of a limited slush fund to get our parts from Nostalgia; so we don't go there often."

"When do we leave?"

"Now, I think this technical speech is too much for you."

Stan gathered their pass cards and computer pads to go to the docking bay. Tobin and Stan walked quickly through the hallways and to the lifts; they moved smooth and efficiently bringing them to the docking bay. This suited Tobin and his impatient attitude.

While in the shuttle navigating close to the red moon "This has to be exciting for you Tobin. Quite the treat I would say." Stan remarked trying to start a conversation.

But his nephew just replied in an unenthusiastic voice "It's not all that great; couldn't they have given us a bigger shuttle. It would be nice to have my own space."

"Sorry kiddo, I don't think you need a whole cabin to yourself. Settle yourself down; the pilot will get us there soon enough. The parts we're picking up are small and just a few of them. So, we don't need a bigger craft."

They sat there quietly staring out the viewing port until they reached a rather basic looking space station. Stan spent the time it took them to get there; thinking about the first couple of times he had met Tobin. He was such a nice little boy easy to pull jokes on, and had a look of brightness on his face and in his eyes. Now Tobin doesn't but have one expression to him; a somber dullness.

Aboard the space station most of the equipment on it looked out dated, and the lights were gloomy. Tobin didn't know whether the station was going to fall apart by just having them step aboard it.

No one seemed to be there just an eerie stillness. Did they come all that way only to go back empty handed? Tobin was about to remark to his uncle about the strange place. When a medium size fellow appeared at one of the entry ways; he wasn't as tall as his uncle. But not quite short either, he was an older man in his late fifty's. He was partially balding and had no facial hair.

The man smiled and said "Welcome! Good to have you here; what can I do for you?"

Stan replied "Sarah arranged for us to pick some parts up for the Gallant."

The man answered "Oh yes, in just a little bit more time I'll have your order around for you. Come follow me to the briefing room."

The group walked down rather old and dingy corridors to come to a fair size plain room. Stan added "Where are my manners Tobin, this is our host Mr. Dent."

Dent replied "Just call me Anthony." As they entered the room, Dent went on to say "I'll have Trace bring you refreshments and check on your order."

Just before Dent left the room Trace entered with a tray of snacks. She was a tall slender woman with green eyes. She had blonde page cut hair. She said to them "I hope these goodies perk you up from your trip. I got them ready ahead of time it would have slipped Anthony's mind."

Stan warmly greeted her with "Good to see you, how is Dent treating you?"

"Quite fine thank you."

"We still need another technician in my department."

"Oh that offer is still there? I don't think you're really trying to fill it."

"It would be worth it to have you on the team."

"Dent keeps me plenty busy and I don't think you could compensate me in the same way."

Tobin quickly tried to find other things to focus his attention on. He noticed the door seem to be ajar; it must have not been making contact with the sensor. Tobin looked at Stan; as he thought he was too far off talking to notice him. Quietly Tobin slipped through the door and to the hallway.

Why does it look so old in here he thought to himself. Does this station have any funds to fix it up to code? How can it still be running in this condition? Tobin let he eyes wander down the hall under the dimming lights. He found his feet following his gaze walking further from the briefing room. As Tobin walked down the hall he noticed the ship seemed to take on different features. There weren't a lot of doors and they seemed to all have code locks on them. With a sigh Tobin thought of going back before he was missed. But with one more look down the hall he noticed another door ajar. Tobin was not a bad natured boy but he didn't want to let the chance of exploring pass him by; after all seldom did anything peek his interest.

When he entered the room it was lowly lit making Tobin uncertain on what to expect. It was packed with small and large crates. It was easy for Tobin to lose his footing as he did, and had to catch himself using a crate. He heard a noise and noticed a shift in the shadows of a corner. Tobin stood up and thought to himself there is something more to this place. Tobin carefully made his way to where he was sure he saw the shift and looked around "Nothing. Great." he said to himself "Hardly worth getting a lecture for." Within a moment he heard another rustle, Tobin panned his eyes back and forth to see if he could catch what made the noise. He found some open crates and start rummaging through them, what he found was almost indescribable to him. Some of the items were extremely out dated and others were unknown to him. He could imagine what they were or what they were ever used for. Old fibers bound together with a form of type on them. What is the purpose of that, all knowledge is digital. Tobin heard the noise again he turned his head in the direction it came from. He seen a shape move to an area he was sure to catch it. Tobin moved quickly and went where he thought it moved to. He peered around a crate and in to a corner. He seen a pair of shinning eyes and a furry outline, Tobin went to creep towards the figure.

"Tobin there you are. I've been looking for you."

Tobin turned around with a surprised look on his face to see Trace. She then said "Come with me. I'll get you back to the briefing room." Tobin followed without saying a word. When they arrived Stan looked sternly at Tobin. Trace said "Oh, I found him. He got lost looking for the ship. You see he went back to get his holo pad."

Stan sternly said "Next time let us know. We could have someone go get it for you." Tobin nodded his head and sat quietly while Stan thanked Trace. Why did she cover up what I was doing? It was like Trace was sticking up for me. She doesn't even know me.

Dent entered the room with a content look on his face. "We managed to find all the parts to fill the order and they are being loaded as we speak. You just have a few minutes to wait and then you can start your trip back." Dent finished saying.

Tobin just wanted to hide, getting on the ship couldn't come quick enough for him. Is this where Trace tells of his mischief? Trace and Dent only exchanged rather pleased expressions.

Stan thanked Dent by saying "Thanks for coming up with the parts for us on short notice. It doesn't seem as though you get to many visitors here."

Dent replied "Oh, we keep ourselves busy in other ways. I guess we can walk you down to your ship." It didn't take the group long to get to the ship. Trace and Dent sent Tobin and Stan off with good tidings.

Tobin was happy to leave without a scolding. Now he had to endure the trip back to the station with his uncle. Stan seemed to be in a pleasant mood. He once again tried to pick up conversation with Tobin. "What did you think of Nostalgia?"

Tobin tried not to give his actions a way. He pretended not to hear his uncle. Stan went on to say "Well I think it was a nice outing from our station. Trace always has something fascinating to talk about. And Dent really knows his stuff, I don't think there is anything that man can't find or get up and running." Stan gave up on talking to Tobin and sat back with a content feeling. He always enjoyed the visits to Nostalgia.

Tobin sat and kept thinking about what he saw back in the storage room. What was all that stuff and that furry animal he seen and where did it come from? For the first time he started to feel an excitement bellowing inside of himself. The ship docked at their home station where the crew began to unload the supplies and parts. Stan and Tobin headed back to the lab to check in with Sarah to verify the parts list. Within a minute the list was done and Stan started to work on the project. He was assigned early that day. Tobin grabbed a chair and sat leaning on the table watching his uncle work. The lab workers offered him some puzzle solving programs to use but Tobin would have nothing to do with it. He would rather be doing something real with his time other than looking at a screen or holo picture.

Nostalgia

Chapter 2

Detective Work

It wasn't too much more time Stan and Tobin were able to go back to their quarters. Stan's first task was to prepare and set for the meal; then he had Tobin began picking up the living area. After a bit Stan called Tobin to dinner they sat and began eating. Tobin looked at Stan and began to think too himself "Uncle really had no idea what I was doing, and I got away with it with no scolding." It was the first time he felt free to do something without the results of being told not to. People on the station were always pushing and directing the youth to grow to be the most productive members of their class. Tobin was different; he wanted to find a different way of doing things and to live a life that was more rewarding to him. Tobin, while lost in thought ate his entire meal to Stan's surprise.

Stan said to Tobin "You won't say it but you did like that little trip of ours. You actually ate all of your meal without having me make you to do so." Tobin came out of his thoughts and looked up at his uncle. He then proceeded to clear the table, ignoring his uncle in his typical fashion.

Stan grinned he had a feeling that things were about to change he just didn't know how." Well I'm going to work on some reports. Make sure you work on those studying programs, I don't need you'll falling behind Tobin." Stan went to his room where he spent most of the remainder of the evening. Tobin did a few chores that were asked of him and afterwards went to his room where he spent the rest of the night thinking about what had gone on that day.

The next two days were back to the same dull life for Tobin. He watched his uncle at work thinking to himself that his uncle was the most boring person alive and hoped never to have a job like his or worse, end up like him. It was about the third day out that Sarah, being frustrated and impatient broke a vital part to their project. Not wanting to wait or let the others know she put in a quick order to Nostalgia. Sarah began to get things arranged for the short trip. She would go on her own making the trip quicker. Stan was on one of the upper decks getting instruments needed for the project. He had left Tobin in the lab with Sarah. Sarah being frantic didn't even remember Tobin being there at all and swiftly jolted out of the room and down the hall with her request form.

Tobin knew it would be awhile before Sarah made it to the shuttle bay. He looked around, all of the other staff members where so wrapped up into their work they didn't notice him being in the room. Tobin couldn't get Nostalgia out of his mind; he had to know more about what was going on at the station. A feeling came over him; the impulse to do what he hadn't done before. Tobin ducked out of the lab without being seen. It was soon to be the shift meal time so most everyone was coming and going. No one would notice him making his way down to the docking bay. Tobin looked around at the ships. Sarah's order was small so it would be the same shuttle his uncle took and it seemed to be the only smaller shuttle in working order. "Yep, that would be the shuttle she would take." Tobin thought. He slipped behind crates and loaders until he got to the shuttle. The pilot was just running the check sheets so he would not have any knowledge of Tobin sneaking on board. There were plenty of cubby holes for him to stowaway in for the short trip. All of this was happening so fast that he wasn't even thinking of the consequences. Sarah quickly boarded the ship and urged the pilot to be swift to complete the order. Tobin sat not making a noise; he listened to the engines that were already warmed up. Thrusters were ignited and the shuttle was off through the bay doors. What was a short trip to Nostalgia seemed to be an eternity for Tobin being tucked away in the dark.

He was relieved when he felt the ship gracefully land in Nostalgia's docking bay. Now he had only to wait for the right moment to creep out of the ship. He planned on leaving the shuttle just long enough to see a little bit of the areas he had not been to. Tobin had questions about what the station really was, he thought for sure they must have been smuggling animals or they got the parts from space pirates. Who would know what happens on this space station? Tobin was going to find out. He peered out the side cabin door there didn't seem to be any one around, not even the pilot. That's strange Tobin thought to himself but convenient for him. Tobin took the passage that they had been on before, this time he was going to take a turn off that he had seen the last time he was on board. He walked swiftly through the empty halls and came to the turn off; Tobin stopped to make sure of his bearings and began to venture down the hall. The interior was unlike the parts of the station he had been in before. Everything seemed to look more modern, was this part of the station updated and the rest hasn't been updated yet? Tobin soon came upon a set of big doors. He looked around and there still seemed to be no other people in the area. He then activated the doors which opened side to side revealing a gigantic docking bay containing ships of different sizes, shapes, styles. Some of them appeared to be older, some current, and others must have been new, because Tobin couldn't identify them. He was astonished never had he ever seen half this much traffic at Nostalgia or at the Gallant. How have they been hiding all this, Tobin had never seen any of these ships leave or dock at the station. People and pilots were mingling as they prepared their ships. Tobin saw people from races he only heard about and some he had never seen or knew existed.

A man with black hair and goatee wearing a black suit came up to Tobin and said "I don't think this is the right place for a little guy like you." The man smiled and put his hand on Tobin's shoulder. "Come with me and I'll take you some place better suiting for you then here." Tobin looked up at him not sure what to do; he decided to follow the man. The man took him to some side doors in the docking bay, where they entered a room. It was a very nice sitting room with a plush couch, chairs, end tables, and plants. The man looked at Tobin and said "My name is Marduc, what would yours be?"

Tobin answered "Tobin."

"Well you're not much of the talking type, are you? I can tell. So you look out of place here. Could it be you're too young to fly a ship?"

Tobin stood there quietly feeling scared and puzzled. Marduc went on to say "Have a seat. So where did you come from and how did you get here."

Tobin defending himself "I don't have to tell you anything. I just took a wrong turn that's all."

"Hmm, let's check in with Dent. He might know where you came from."

Tobin walked over and sat in one of the chairs, he watched Marduc to see what he would do. Marduc said to Tobin "I'll be back to see what I can do with you."

Marduc left the room with a smirk on his face. Tobin thought to himself, what all this could be and how much trouble he was going to be in? It was only a short while and Marduc was back with Dent.

Dent looked at Tobin and said "Tobin how did you get here? Oh, did you sneak and stow away on the ship Sarah came on? Did you?"

Tobin answered "Yes."

"Well, then you should know Sarah has the parts she ordered and already departed to go back to the station."

"What are you going to do with me? What's really going on here, this isn't a normal supply station?"

"I'll be sending you back to your uncle. About this station; it supplies its customers with what they need. Anything above that is none of your concern."

"If you're doing something illegal I'll put a stop to it."

"That's some sass coming from a little boy living in a shell. There is nothing illegal going on here; it's just a complicated operation to explain. For now I would like to see you safe with your uncle. On your next trip here I'll explain and show you what's going on. I assure you we are doing legitimate operations."

"You'll have me come back?"

"I'll have you back with your uncle for now. It is not right to run off on him like you did."

"Oh….."

"Lessons are learned in time. Marduc would you please make sure Tobin is taken back to the Gallant promptly. I have other things to attend to."

Marduc replied "Why yes, I will." He smiled at Tobin and said "Come on little guy lets go."

Tobin nodded and left with Marduc to the bay. They stopped at a small craft. Marduc remarked "We'll take one of Nostalgia's shuttles, although my ship is much better than this one."

Tobin gave a little smirk; he was becoming fond of Marduc. The man seemed to have a style about him and appeared to like Tobin. The two of them loaded up into the shuttle and were on their way to the Gallant. Tobin could see all the stars and station from the viewing window. He felt he had a little more appreciation for the view. Tobin asked Marduc "How do you know Dent; are you a customer of his?"

Marduc replied "I and Dent are old colleagues from a long time back. Now days I check up on him and pick up parts from him. He gave me the nick name M, but seldom uses it."

"So, you two are close friends?"

"Yes, you can say we are. We have been to a lot of places together at different times."

"Was he all ways so dull and old looking?"

"At one time he was young but he has never been dull. You just haven't seen the real him yet."

The ship was getting close to the Gallant and Tobin saw what he thought to be the shuttle Sarah took earlier to go to Nostalgia. Was she leaving again or was someone else using the shuttle Tobin pondered? Tobin then asked Marduc "Am I going to be in big trouble when I get back?"

Marduc responded "I would imagine you would be in trouble." Within moments the shuttle docked and Tobin exited the shuttle. Marduc went up and talked to the docking clerk and came back to Tobin. "Well. You're all set; you better find your uncle. I hope to see you again soon." Marduc smiled and shook Tobin's hand. Then entered the shuttle and prepared to leave.

Tobin reluctantly headed back to the lab to meet up with his uncle. The halls still seemed to be busy with people coming and going. Tobin thought it must have been time for the shift change. It must be late his uncle was sure going to be giving him a talking to and then some. Tobin did care about the scolding. He ignores the talking but the hurt feelings that would be left behind are the parts Tobin wasn't looking forward to having. He was getting close to the lab when he seen his uncle walking towards him.

Stan came up to Tobin and asked "There you are, you ready to get some lunch to eat?"

Tobin responded "Yes."

The two of them walked together to the food service hall. Tobin was thrown to see his uncle in a good mood. Did he know about were Tobin was, doesn't he know he's supposed to be giving a lecture? Tobin and

Stan were served their food and went to seat themselves.

Stan started a conversation by saying "I guess Sarah went to get replacement parts and left you by yourself. Shame on her, I knew you would start to wander if I didn't leave you with supervision. Oh well, no harm done."

Tobin inquiringly said "Did they serve lunch late?"

"No, it's served right on time. You must have lost track of time." Stan said with a slight look of bewilderment about his face.

Tobin was fairly sure he was gone for a long time. After a short pause He asked "Did Sarah come back with her parts?"

Stan replied "No she's still out getting them, last I knew."

Tobin paused and thought; how could that be? Was Dent lying to him, I couldn't be back that quick?

Stan looked at Tobin and said "You know I did get a message from Dent…" Tobin stared at his uncle. Stan went on to finish his statement to Tobin "You really must have impressed him. Dent asked me if you could come to his station and do some work for him. He said you could consider it a field trip. I told him that I would ask you first before I could give him an answer. So, what do you think?" Stan asked with an enthusiastic tone.

Tobin was baffled but in order to find out what was happening on Nostalgia, he was going to have to accept the offer. Tobin nodded to his uncle and said "Yes, I would like to. It's way better than sitting in the lab all day."

Stan obligingly said "I'll make sure to message him and let him know you'll start at the beginning of the week."

After lunch they went back to the lab. Stan had decided to make it a short day and took Tobin back to their quarters. The first thing Stan did was message Dent using the holo transmitter. Stan then told Tobin "Everything is setup. When it is time for you to go, Dent will send a shuttle for you." Tobin nodded in agreement with what his uncle had said.

Tobin and Stan went on to do their regular routines for the evening. As Tobin went to sleep that night he couldn't help but wonder what was going to happen; and what he was going to see at Nostalgia? It was just a few short days later and Tobin was waiting in the shuttle bay. He couldn't believe his uncle was just going to let him leave for a week.

Marduc

Chapter 3

The Shop

In just a while of waiting the shuttle from Nostalgia arrived. Tobin was glad to see Marduc was the pilot of it. Marduc exited the shuttle and greeted Tobin. He looked at Tobin's bag and said "Tobin you ready to go? Wait, that bag isn't going to be enough for the trip."

Tobin replied briskly "It will be plenty. My things are air sealed."

"I suppose it might do then. Let's load up and get going." Marduc replied with a quizzical tone.

Tobin gave his bag to Marduc and entered the shuttle. Marduc seated Tobin and began to navigate back to Nostalgia. Tobin asked Marduc "What will I be doing when we get to the station?"

Marduc answered "I'm not exactly sure? I would think that Dent will give you a proper tour of the station for starters."

"Will you be working with me for the week?" inquired Tobin.

"I'll stop to see you, but I'm a customer my boy not a resident of Nostalgia."

"Is Dent really going to have me work for him?" asked Tobin timidly.

"Yes, I believe so and he'll get hard work out of you. You kind of owe him after all Dent covered up your little stow away trip." Marduc said with a chuckle.

"How did he do that? I thought it to be impossible to get me back like he did."

"That's a secret Dent is going to have to tell you himself. After all I wouldn't want to spoil it for you. You were trying to be a detective and find out what's going on for yourself. You wouldn't learn anything if I did it for you now would you?" Marduc retorted mysteriously.

"Detective Tobin…. I like the idea." Tobin mused to himself.

"We're going to dock at Nostalgia. Ready yourself."

The shuttle landed in the bigger bay with all the coming and going traffic. When Tobin and Marduc left the shuttle they were greeted by Dent and Trace. Trace wasn't wearing her normal work suit; she had a blouse and skirt made out of a thick grey material. Dent was wearing a full three piece suit. It was black and had a white ruffled shirt different from his plainer straight looking suit he wore before during Tobin's last visit. The two of them looked out of place. Come to think of it so was the way Marduc was dressed.

Dent smiled at Tobin and said "Glad to see you again. I hope you'll settle in well here."

Trace added "It was good of you to come."

Tobin spoke confidently "Dent and my uncle

agreed I should come here, I have an obligation to fill."

Dent chuckled "Come then, I'll show you around the station to the parts you haven't seen. The rest of Nostalgia is more interesting than just its storage rooms."

Tobin, Trace, and Marduc followed Dent to an elevator were they all entered. Dent used the key pad sending them into an upward motion to the higher decks. They stopped on level a 12. Dent said to Tobin "This floor will be where your room for your stay is. Follow me." They went down the hall just a ways, and stopped at the first set of doors. Dent and Tobin went in to the room. Dent then explained "I know it's rather small quarters, but it will be just fine for a young boy. Come then, leave your bag we have better things to see."

Tobin left his bag and followed Dent back to the others. They went up one level in the elevator. Dent asked Tobin "Are you ready for this?"

Tobin nodded his head. The doors opened to reveal a vast room full of shelves with items Tobin had never seen before. There were statues, paintings and racks of clothes; all kinds of weird looking things. It was enormous with balconies reaching all through it, the parts that had shelves looked like a storage area. The area that had clothing racks looked like the clothing center on the Gallant. There was a section that looked arty and was meant to resemble a museum. The walls were bright and had liquid colorful lights to illuminate everything to be seen. The floor had parts of it as tile and other sections as carpet. There was an elegant stair case that went up to a platform that had locked cases. On a large shelve was a four person boat. How did Dent get that in here and the rest of this stuff Tobin thought?

Tobin puzzled said "What does a bunch of junk

have to do with anything?"

Dent disappointedly said "I thought you had a keener mind then the rest of your people. Are you going to prove me wrong?"

"I didn't mean what I said. I meant what is the use of all these items? What would anyone do with all of this stuff?" Tobin spoke flustered by Dent's words.

"That is the start of it. You Tobin are going to tag and catalog all of these items." Said Dent with a reassuring demeanor in his voice.

"Not in a week, you would need the whole station to do that." Tobin grumbled.

"We'll see if you can. Enough, let's get you started on your task. You can see the rest of the station later." Dent stated in a rushed manner.

Marduc interrupted the two by saying "I bid you ado for now Tobin. I'll see you another time perhaps." Spoke Marduc as he gave a nod to Tobin and a wink to Dent and Trace.

Tobin, Dent, and Trace exited the elevator leaving Marduc within to make use of it. Marduc smiled as the doors closed making Tobin feel unsure about things with him leaving.

Dent went on to say "Let's go to the heart of the room." They walked through the room stopping at a counter with an old looking computer box. Dent continuing his speech "This is the register where our customers will check out."

Tobin still puzzled asked "Why would anyone buy this stuff?"

Dent answered "They need them for the right time."

"Time for what exactly?" inquired Tobin, a bit perplexed.

"The time they will be going to." Dent said reassuringly.

"You don't go to time you go to places." Tobin stated confidently.

"Yes, places in time." Dent corrected.

"You don't need this stuff now, why would you need it at any other time?" Tobin stated, now beginning to question what Dent was saying.

"If you are going to that time, you'll need them then." Dent stated with a sense of urgency underlying his smile.

"I give up." Tobin said as he threw his arms up in defeat.

Trace smiled and giggled "Let me try." She said. "When your uncle was young he dressed different from what you dress now."

Tobin agreed "Right."

"If you go back to play with your uncle when he was a young boy you would look different to him." Trace implored.

"But I'm not and why would I" Tobin said, still looking at both Trace and Dent with doubt in his eyes.

"If you traveled time you would." Trace asked.

"If I could travel time I would go someplace far better than to see my uncle as a kid. Wait a minute this isn't some kind of school lesson is it?" Tobin asked with a raised brow.

Dent answered "You will learn much but not from programs. You will learn what time periods all this stuff came from and meet the people going there."

Tobin said perplexed "Time travelers, do they exist?"

"You should know; you yourself did." Dent stated nonchalantly.

"That could have been the only way you could have gotten me back without being in trouble." Tobin quietly spoke as all the puzzle pieces began to align in his mind's eye.

"I thought you were smart but you made me spell it out for you." Dent calmly spoke.

"A detective has to have a confession." Tobin stated coyly.

"At least you're sharp. Tobin, I sell parts to fix and maintain time machines."

"And space stations." Trace added.

"Yes, for your station there are vintage parts I don't use for my station any more. I decided that I was going to sell to the time travelers what they need to fit in to where they are going. You do follow, don't you?"

"I'm still stuck on real time travelers. Where did you get all this stuff?" Tobin asked with an awakened sense of wonderment.

"I'm a bit of a hoarder. Selling this stuff would be a big help to me actually." Dent said sheepishly.

"Pirates are so out and crazy old man is in." Tobin stated with a smirk.

"You're a tad bit mean like your uncle said you would be." Dent replied.

Trace interjected "I'll be going; I have other things to attend to. I think the two of you will get along just fine without me." Trace walked away from the two and seemed to disappear in the racks of items.

Tobin looked at Dent and said "So you really travel time then?"

Dent answered "Yes, but I thought I would settle in to one place for a while."

"Why doesn't every one time travel?" Tobin asked, still trying to comprehend the full scope of all he had just learned

"A lot of people do, there is just a restriction or two on it."

"Can you go anywhere you want?" Tobin implored.

"A time traveler is restricted to certain times and places. That is so they don't upset the balance of things." Dent said.

"What because there is a time hall monitor or something?" Tobin said sarcastically.

"Why yes, something like that."

"Who are they?" Tobin asked dumbfounded

"You'll know when you meet them. They are called T.W.C." Dent said with an air of importance to the statement.

"You just took the fun out of time travel." Tobin stated with a sigh.

"It's time to stop talking and start working. We'll begin by labeling items from your time so you don't get lost. Follow me carefully, onward this way. Each item will be labeled by description, place, and time it came from. Then we will add a code to scan the item when it's ready for sale. When the traveler goes to buy the item they must scan their travel card. If they are not meant to go to that time the computer will reject the sale. You follow me on this? OK." inquired Dent.

"Yes, how do I know where the item is from?" Tobin asked.

"In the desk there is an index you can look them up by description or take a guess to find what the items are. I'll show you how to do it for a bit and then I'll have you do it on your own."

Dent showed Tobin the steps and the two of them worked on it for some time. It was easy for Tobin to catch on, because he knew about the clothes, tech, and what they were for. Dent finally said "That will be a day for us I'll take you to the dining hall."

Tobin relieved to hear this said "Sounds good. It's been awhile since I've eaten."

Tobin and Dent entered the elevator and was shuttled to another deck on the station. Unlike the last deck Tobin had been on this one was full of people coming and going. All shapes, sizes, colors, and even furry beings were there. The deck was more open you could see into rooms, which appeared to be stores. Was this a big shopping center; like they have on other planets Tobin thought to himself? They came to the dining hall where they were greeted and seated by the host. Dent let Tobin know he would order the food and the next time they came Tobin could try other types of food if he liked.

Tobin asked "Do you serve food from other planets?"

Dent answered "Yes, the finest you'll ever find."

"What about food from different time periods then?"

"Yes, though it's tricky to do. When transporting food it will tend to spoil; if you go through the wrong time rift." Dent replied with a wink.

"Are all these people and beings time travelers?" Tobin asked, with wonderment.

"Most of them are time travelers or they at least have a good concept of space and time albeit a limited concept."

"So, why I'm I here?" Tobin inquired, voice slightly cracking with anticipation.

"To help me, setup my antique shop of course." Dent stated nonchalantly.

"Alright………" Tobin said in a questioning quiet manner.

"You're doing fine don't worry." Reassured Dent to his wide eyed new ward.

The two of them finished their food and departed to the elevator. Dent walked Tobin to his quarters and wished him well for the night. "I'll come get you after you have rested." Dent told Tobin and then he was about his business else were.

Jessy

Chapter 4

A Ghost and New Friend

Tobin looked over his quarters and room it was much nicer than the one he has with his uncle. Tobin unpacked his things and lay back on the bed. He thought about all the wonderful things he seen. In truth he liked being on board Nostalgia. He hoped the next day would be just as exciting. It didn't seem long before Tobin heard a buzzing noise at the door. He got up and opened the door to see Dent.

Who began to say "Good god do you plan to sleep all day? Go get yourself ready. I'll meet you in the dining hall." Tobin nodded and Dent was on his way.

Tobin was confused it seemed as if he just gotten to sleep. He got cleaned and dressed then headed down to the dining hall. Dent was already seated with breakfast ready for Tobin.

Dent opened the conversation with "I made sure to order you a big breakfast you'll need it. You should set your alarm though; I won't be able to come get you up every morning."

Tobin asked "What time is it?"

"Eight a.m." Dent said in a rushed manner.

"Should I set the alarm for seven?" Tobin asked, still trying to shake off the haze of sleep still encompassing him.

"That would do fine?" Dent replied in a mild demeanor.

After breakfast Tobin and Dent went to the shop. Dent setup up items for Tobin to work on that he had no idea what they were. Come midday Dent left and came back with lunch for Tobin. Tobin thanked him and began to ask questions about the items they were cataloging. Tobin listened intently to the stories about places and times he had never been himself. Tale after tale was told as Tobin held on to every word. One story in particular grabbed Tobin's attention. I was a tale of a cursed book and it's abilities to open rifts in the very fabric of time.

"I have a cautionary story about a fellow I know named Jack. You see my boy, he had stumbled across an item that he had no idea how to use. He had traveled time so much after awhile he himself was lost." Dent stated with a smile.

Tobin's eyes widen, "Please continue."

"A yes, now where was I? That's right it's all coming back to me now. He's gone by many a name over the years. From a cabin in the woods to shores of ancient seas, he never knew where nor when the book would take him or how long he would be. Be he known as Ashley, a nobleman, or a hack. I shall forever know his as a fellow named Jack." Dent gleamed.

Tobin looked at Dent with amazement from such a tale.

"So have I met him or will I meet him?" implored Tobin.

Dent replied to Tobin with a shake of his head "I'm afraid to say Tobin you haven't made his acquaintance yet; you don't know Jack."

Tobin's mind was pondering all the stories Dent had told him and had almost forgotten to eat his lunch. Such stories and such places. After lunch Dent left Tobin on his own to work.

Tobin grew bored of the work; the room became to quite for him. Everything there was new to him and he found himself playing and fiddling with the items. As Tobin was daydreaming about what the items were for and who would have used them, a scurrying noise snapped him out of his own little world. Tobin lifted his head to pan his gaze around the room. He spotted a long coat moving and without hesitation began to creep up on it. He pulled away the coat to reveal a purple with blackish highlights furry mouse looking animal. It had a glowing bulbous looking thing on the end of its tail. It must have stood a foot and a half tall and had big orange eyes. It blinked its eyes, wrinkled its nose, and tried to climb back into the coat. Tobin quickly grabbed at the coat where he thought the critter would be cautious not to hurt the animal.

Luck was with him; Tobin managed to get a firm grasp on it. He then began to say "It's OK little guy, I'm not going to hurt you. Shh, be quiet now." Tobin pulled the little one out of its hiding place. He held it firmly and stroked its head. "Now, now, there no one who is going to hurt you. You are going to be all right." Tobin's cooing and talking seemed to calm down the critter. "Well you're a little cutie aren't you? I wonder where you came from." The animal relaxed and began to enjoy the attention Tobin gave it. Tobin gave it a snack he had tucked in his pocket he was saving. The little animal ate it and seemed to like it. "So, we're friends then?" asked Tobin.

Tobin heard a voice say "There you are. Oh, you found one of them." He looked up to see Dent standing there staring at him.

Tobin responded "What is it?"

"It's called a Ferishen it's in the rodent family. They're considered to be a pest, but then I'm sure you'll think its cutie."

Tobin looked at Dent and opened his eyes as wide as he could. "It warmed up to me." Tobin said cheerfully.

"I see you're going to want to keep it aren't you?" Dent asked.

"If it's no trouble while I'm here on Nostalgia." Tobin implored.

"Let's take a look at it. Well, now he is going to be your responsibility. And remember it's a boy." chuckled Dent.

"OK, he'll stay out of trouble. I'll feed and watch him while I work." Promised Tobin

"You don't even know what it eats." Dent stated with an uplifting tone.

"I'm sure it might be in one of your logs." Tobin coyly stated.

"It eats most everything." Dent stated with a reassuring nod.

"So, how far have you gotten since I left Tobin?"

"A couple of years' worth I think." said Tobin timidly.

"Keep up the good work. I'll stay with you until dinner and then we'll get your little friend some food."

Tobin's new found friend stayed close to him while he worked. It watched his every move. Dent had Tobin put it in a carrying bag when they went to eat so that the little critter wouldn't upset anyone. Upon leaving they got an extra order of food so Tobin could bring it with him for the Ferishen.

As Dent went to leave Tobin at his quarters he asked "What are you going to name him for the time that you have to spend with him?"

Tobin responded with "Jessy."

"That doesn't sound like a pet's name."

"He's not my pet." Said Tobin

Tobin opened and looked into the bag and smiled. He then entered his quarters, closed the doors behind him, leaving Dent in the hall. Tobin took the bag and sat it on the bed tipping it on its side letting the Ferishen slowly come out. He then took the food and placed it on the bed for the critter. The little one was quite happy to receive the food and wasted no time eating it. "There Jessy isn't that better." Tobin said and went on to say to the Ferishen "I bet you were the one I seen in the storage room. Huh." Tobin petted and played with Jessy until he fell asleep. The Ferishen made Tobin happy; up to this point in life Tobin didn't have any friends. For once in his life he had something more than four walls and ceiling. He had another being to share his existence with. He finally felt something beyond just life he was given.

      The next day Tobin was up promptly and headed out for breakfast without being prodded by Dent. He ordered extra food and after eating was off to catalog so as to get Jessy his food without being bothered. Dent showed up after him and was pleased to see Tobin so proactive. After a while Dent left Tobin on his own, so as to do other things. Tobin spent part of his day working and part of it playing. He found himself enjoying all the facts and knowledge he was learning about places and times. The items were unique and it made Tobin want to see all of the places they had come from.

      As he was working Tobin was surprised to find a woman standing behind a shelf. He then asked her "Who are you and why are you here?"

      The woman answered "Chrissy and I'm helping catalog items here."

      Tobin didn't know what to think of her as he hadn't seen her before. He then said "I've been here for a better part of a week and I haven't seen you working on this at all."

      Chrissy replied "Oh, dear I've been here the whole time helping. You just don't quite know how to think and see in to the fourth dimension yet. I'm sure you will though. I don't think you'll be seeing me too much. You and I will get the work done and it will be fantastic." Chrissy stated, in an almost sterile manner.

      "What do you mean, how can that be?" Tobin asked, more inquisitive about her statement.

      "It will sink into that noggin of yours." Chrissy said, tone unchanged by Tobin's inquiry.

The lady seemed to disappear as Tobin went to say "What's that mean?" He couldn't believe what he just seen. She must have been a ghost he thought. When Tobin went to eat with Dent he told him what had happened.

Dent wasn't surprised and told Tobin "Chrissy is helping us with the inventory."

Tobin in shock said "She must be a ghost."

"You could say that, but she really is just on a different time stream then we are." Dent paused and then finished with "I guess it would make her a like ghost to us."

"I'm inventorying with a ghost." Tobin said with a slight bit of fleeting fear in his voice.

"You did want to know what goes on here. And I know you want something that isn't your normal boring life. Right…" Dent said, with a slightly coy smirk.

"Yes, but you leave me with more than enough why's and needing to know more than I am told." implored Tobin.

"And that is what will make you great. Shall we go?" Dent said as he gathered up there luncheon trays to heading to their collection repository.

"Yes." Tobin mumbled with a shrug.

Back at his quarters Tobin thought about the week being almost over and what other strange things would happen. Tobin continued his work routine for the rest of the week. On what he thought would be his last day Tobin was preparing himself to say goodbye to Jessy. When Dent came to get Tobin, he had half his things ready to go.

Dent looked at him and said "Why are you packing? The work is not done yet."

Tobin puzzled said "It's been a week; you told my uncle you would bring me back after a week."

"A week in his time line, yes. If it is OK with you I would like to have you work for me longer. I can arrange for you to have the time to." Dent stated mysteriously.

"I guess I can, it would give me more time to spend with Jessy." Tobin said excitedly.

"Well off you go, you can take care of your things later." Dent said as he departed.

Later that day, as Dent and Tobin were having lunch. Tobin asked "Will my uncle notice that I have stayed longer than a week."

Dent answered "He wouldn't notice as long as the time that you're gone doesn't extend past a month to three months. After that he would tell something was up. It really all depends on how fast you grow. For an adult it is harder to notice the difference time takes on them."

"Is this like a summer vacation?" Tobin asked, just a smidge bewildered.

"You can say that, except you're working." Dent replied with his index fingers upon his lips as though he was pondering.

"It doesn't feel like it. I'm having more fun than if I had stayed with my uncle." Tobin said with a twinge of excitement in his voice.

"I'm happy to hear that, it means you'll be very productive." Dent said with glee.

After lunch Dent helped Tobin work for the rest of the day. Tobin started to spend more time walking around the station and getting familiar with the decks and the people on them; Jessy also enjoyed the walks. On one day while Tobin was cataloging he ran into a problem. A statue he had tagged seemed to have been moved. This became a frustrating for him after the third time cataloging the statue. Tobin went and brought Dent over to show it to him and once again it had moved.

Dent explained "You see that is what we call a golem. They are blood tied to their master; this one is missing his and waiting for a new one."

Tobin curiously said "What is it supposed to do for its master?"

"Anything he or she tells it to do." Dent said.

"I don't think you should be selling it, it could hurt someone." Tobin stated with a concerned tone.

"It's OK to sell it to the right person." Dent spoke.

"That makes no sense." Tobin said still alarmed by this revelation.

"By the by, Marduc will be visiting tomorrow." Dent said as he hastily departed.

"You do know how to change the subject." Tobin shot out towards Dent.

"Just go with the flow. He'll be picking up some items." Dent spoke over his shoulder as he walked away.

"Do you need help getting them ready?" shouted Tobin down the aisle.

"No, but I'm sure you would like to visit with him." Dent said as he turned to look back at Tobin.

"I would." Tobin acknowledged.

Dent went to work at the register; Tobin looked at the golem and said "I'm watching you. No funny business."

Dent

Chapter 5

Run Away

The next day Dent had Tobin took the morning off so he could spend it with Marduc exploring Nostalgia and learning more about time travel. Tobin was able to see computers that were more advanced than the ones on his own space station. Marduc showed and explained to him about different space ships, shuttles, and space freighters. They had lunch together and then Marduc took Tobin back to the shop. While there Marduc picked up a crystal of sorts that Tobin had already tagged and cataloged.

Marduc commented, "I'll need this I've already cleared it with Dent."

Tobin looked puzzled and said "That will make my job harder; I just logged that not long ago."

"Don't mind about it; just clear it from your logs. Oh, by the way here's a shuttle manual you can have to study from; the manual is to a shuttle just like the one Nostalgia has." Marduc quickly stated as he passed the manual to Tobin.

Tobin took the manual and said "Thanks for the manual. Are you sure it's OK with Dent?"

"Yes, it will be fine. I have to be going now. You take care of yourself and your little friend." Marduc stated with a wink.

"I have work I need to get back to. Bye for now."

Marduc smiled and left with the crystal in hand. After Marduc was on the elevator and gone Tobin was surprised by Chrissy.

Chrissy spoke "Sorry to startle you. I just wanted to say there something up with Marduc. I just don't trust him."

Tobin with a tone of disbelief said, "I don't know you well; and you think I should trust what you say?"

"If I was not to be trusted don't you think I would have done something to you by now?" Chrissy replied in a quizzical manner.

"True, what is Marduc up to?" Tobin pondered.

"You're just a little boy I don't want you to learn mistrust in people so early on in life."

"So why say anything about it to me?" inquired Tobin.

"To help me in case I need you. I don't think Dent would believe me. Marduc and Dent go way back as friends. A tight bond I think, but it still bothers me. I see him doing things that seem harmless and I can't put together what he is doing." Chrissy said in a low tone.

She was looking down towards her feet and fidgeting with her fingers as she felt as though perhaps she had said too much.

"As long as he isn't hurting anything it should be OK. I hate to lose a friend over a small matter." Tobin said with sincerity in his voice.

"It'll all work out I'm sure. You know you're doing a good job inventorying." Chrissy stuttered, trying to change the topic.

"I think you're trying to get on my good side." Tobin said with a mischievous grin.

Chrissy smiled and drifted away like smoke. Tobin thought "Could his new friend Marduc be up to no good?" He decided to be quite about the matter. After all Tobin had a good judgment on peoples characters. But he would keep an eye on things while on Nostalgia. Nothing about Marduc or anything being missing was mentioned at all by Dent. Tobin let everything be, it seemed as if everything would be OK. A good chunk of the work was done and Tobin decided to slow down a little bit and start reading the manual he was given.

Upon cataloging Tobin ran across a large blue box, it wasn't anywhere in that sections logs or time. So Tobin went to go find Dent and ask him about it. When he found him, Dent was talking to a short dark haired man wearing a fur coat. Tobin came up to them listening and watching what was going on. The strange man was saying to Dent "I'll pay you well more than what it is worth."

Dent replied "It's the principle of it. My shop is not officially open yet and you don't have an active card."

"Why should that matter?" inquired the man as his eyes darted about the room.

"I will not lose a license I have not yet gotten and

certainly over you wanting a bauble of sorts!" Dent said in a slightly raised voice.

"Does it really matter?" asked the man as he fiddled with his coat.

"Yes! Now off with you." Dent pointed towards the entry way.

The strange man gave a huff and walked away into the racks. Tobin asked Dent "Who was that?"

Dent answered "So, who isn't as good at time as they think they are."

"That makes no sense. I have to show you something out of place." Tobin said as he scratched his head.

"I'll come with you, but if you think truly about it my boy, everything here is out of place." Dent chuckled.

"You like to give me grief over anything you can?" asked Tobin.

"It's the boss's job."

Tobin took Dent to where he had seen the box just to see it was gone. Tobin sighed and said "I shouldn't be surprised, nothing stays put around here."

Dent asked, "What did it look like Tobin?"

"It was a big blue box." Tobin attempted to add emphasis by using his hands to show its girth.

"That wasn't one of mine and I'm sure it will be back." Dent added with a nod.

"I'll take your word for it." Tobin grumbled as he

shook his head in disbelief.

After that things kept moving ahead. The closer the shop came to being done the more Dent became happier and the sadder Tobin got. On one day Tobin felt heart broke at the thought of leaving Nostalgia. So, he stayed in his quarters for the day. Tobin only ate snacks he had saved from the other day. He played with Jessy feeling his warm fur between his fingers as he petted him. Tobin didn't want to leave, there was so much more to learn and so many more people to meet. Being on Nostalgia to Tobin was living a life, doing something that meant something to someone. Going back to the Gallant would just seem so bland in comparison.

Working in the shop had so much color to it and living back with his uncle everything was water down feeling. His attention fell on the manual and why he would have it? Parts of it were easy to understand and then others were beyond him. Tobin pickup and read the manual on and off through the day. Every detail he could ever want to know or would ever need to know was in this manual. A bit advanced for him but a gift from a friend beat a holo lesson any day. Towards the end of the day Dent came to see Tobin.

Dent inquired about Tobin's acts by saying "You decided you were not going to work today?"

Tobin answered "What's the point when your shop is ready you'll send me back to my uncle."

"Wait, you the boy who hates everything, wants to stay here?" Dent said perplexed.

"Yes."

"I'm not your family and I'm not going to raise

you." Dent stated firmly.

"I like it here I feel like I belong." Tobin softly said as his eyes got misty

"I'll have to take you back when it is time; but I can always have you come back to visit at another time." Dent said with a hint of sadness.

"OK, then." Tobin acknowledged.

"So, tomorrow morning then, bright and early right?" Dent asked, trying to lighten the mood.

"Yes." Tobin said in a low utterance.

Before Dent left he gave Tobin more Snacks knowing it was close to dinner. Tobin didn't know why Dent was so nice to him; he never did anything to earn it from him. As long as Tobin could remember every time he stayed some place long enough to like it he had to leave. His parents were always going someplace and never staying with him. It's the reason Tobin pretends to hate his uncle and everyone on the station. He made himself believe by hating everyone it would make it so he wouldn't have to leave. He thought if he was unhappy it meant he wouldn't have to be alone. After much thought and a night of restless sleep, Tobin got up early and went to the shop.

Dent and Chrissy greet him when he arrived; Dent spoke first "You ready Tobin?"

Tobin quickly said "Yeah."

"You are a special part of this project." Dent stated with a proud smile.

"It's OK, I understand. I'm just happy to have a

break from the Gallant." Tobin said in frigid tone.

Chrissy encouragingly said "You can work with me for the day."

Chrissy took Tobin by the shoulder and lead him to the racks that they would be working on that day. Tobin asked "Why is it that you can stay longer this time with me than last?"

Chrissy answered "Nostalgia in a time space drift caused by a storm; it is on more than one time line and in perpetual movement on multidimensional plains. In other terms it's like layers in a planet. The time lines are getting closer together right now and you'll be seeing more of me."

"I'd like that." Tobin said, finally starting to shake off his melancholy.

"I'd like that to; you're a good kid." Chrissy said with a smile.

The next week or so everyone went out of their way to show how much they appreciated Tobin's help. Tobin felt they were just putting on a good face for him. He had continued to catalog and read the manual in his spare time. Being on Nostalgia was a wonderful place, how could he leave it? Tobin also asked himself the question how could his parents have left him alone all those years ago? He tried to remember how old he was and everything about his parents. He was told they were lost but Tobin would always think whether or not they did want to come back for him. What if I could go someplace and not leave and be happy? Tobin thought this and other things to himself, mind swirling over infinite possibilities.

It did come for the day the shop was to be open to all the time travelers. Chrissy, Trace, Tobin, and Dent were there to open the shop. Everyone was excited, but Tobin wasn't sure what to think or feel. Tobin asked if Dent told anyone they were to open and he answered with "No."

Tobin confused said "How will anyone know to come?"

"They just will." Dent said, with a hint of confidence in his voice.

And with that people indeed started coming. Trace ran the register, Dent guided customers to the items they needed. Chrissy and Tobin answered questions and brought items to the register for the people. Tobin was astonished to see what people were buying. Someone even bought a cursed contract; Tobin thought no one would ever do that. Who wants a cursed item; could you use it and if so what for? The man with the fur coat came back with a young gentle man following him. And the only thing he bought was a flute. Nothing added up to Tobin why anyone would travel space and time for any of this stuff. Tobin stopped a person and asked what they would do with the item? The person said a duchess needed the brooch and if he gave it to her, she would in turn help him. Tobin came to the conclusion Dent knew these people were going to need these items.

"How smart is that." Tobin said to himself. He was happy to be a part of everything going on; it was a purpose that meant something. He found himself idolizing Dent and wanting to be like him. Tobin worked selling to and helping customers at the shop for the next week. He got to hear different stories and met the strangest people. The last night of the week Tobin lay in bed looking at the ceiling. He knew what he wanted in life and it was to be like Dent, a time traveler.

He sat up and looked at Jessy and said "Come with me little guy, we're leaving." Tobin grabbed his bag and put Jessy in to it, and started his way down Nostalgia's hallways. He was used to the stations layout and knew what pathways were less used. He made his way to the shuttle bay and there was not a soul in sight. Strange but Tobin wasn't going to miss the opportunity to get to Nostalgia's shuttle. Once in the shuttle he observed it looked just like the manual's diagram. Tobin earlier that week looked up a planets coordinate's that he thought would be a good start for his new life. He programmed the coordinates into the shuttles console.

Tobin came out of the shuttle to set the auto control system for the bay doors on the docking bay's console, it was something he picked up from his studies on the Gallants operations. He then went back into the shuttle strapped himself in and secured Jessy in as well. The bay started its program, Tobin then started the shuttle. From this point out Tobin shouldn't have to do any manual operating of the controls. He watched the air locks initialize and the bay doors open. The shuttle lifted as Tobin watched the console to make sure it was going through the initialize process. The shuttle navigated its way out the bay; Tobin turned his head to look out the back viewing screen and watched the station drift into the background of stars.

"Wow, we're really doing it." Tobin said to Jessy. He sat back for quite a while watching the instruments. Everything seemed to be going fine; they passed the moon and then the Gallant. Tobin got up, walked around, and started taking inventory of what was in the shuttle after all he wasn't sure how long the trip was going to be. He didn't have rations packed so he was going to rely on what was on the ship and hoped Nostalgia's crew kept things prepared in case of long trips. The inventory looked good they must have been expecting to use the shuttle; because Tobin had found a case marked Gallant with instruments in it. All would be good for the trip he just hoped he didn't need landing codes. Tobin went back to the pilot's seat to see how far they had come. When he seen the consoles panel he couldn't understand it was reading that they were almost to their destination.

Tobin looked out the viewing screen to see the Gallant. He was sure the panel must be broken it brought them into a complete circle. Could it be that he put the wrong code in. Just then the Gallant messaged the shuttle. Tobin answered the voice and it said "Ah, you must have brought the instruments we asked for. The chief will be happy you saved her a trip."

Tobin replied "Yes, all is well and we have your case of instruments ready for you. I hope you don't mind a student delivering it."

The voice said "OK, then you'll be ready to land momentarily."

Tobin hoped whoever was on the shifts leader of the bay didn't recognize him. He thought to himself, he was in hot water. Tobin had no idea how long after his first week at Nostalgia he would be showing up at the Gallant. This was going to mess up Dent's entire time traveler identity and the thought made Tobin regretful. After the shuttle landed Tobin grabbed Jessy, along with the case, and headed out the door. The bay seemed to look as if it was remodeled, a lot must have gone on sense he left. The shift leader came up to him not knowing who he was and thanked him for bringing the case and invited Tobin to stay and refresh himself before going back to Nostalgia. Tobin agreed and then started to make his way to his and his uncle's quarters. He hoped his uncle would be gone, so Tobin could get a grasp on what date it was by looking at his holo computer. When he gotten there he saw a man enter his quarters. As Tobin walked up to the door a girl opened it and came out. She looked at him and asked him who he was.

Tobin said "I'm Tobin and I live here."

The girl replied "Oh no, I have lived here for months now. You must be lost, all these halls and doors look the same. Can I help you find your quarters?"

Tobin "OK. By the way what's the time and day? The instruments in the shuttle I arrived on had malfunctioned."

Her response gave Tobin's head a whirl; he was eleven years in the past. The girl started to walk ahead of him to lead him down the hall. She looked back to see him gone. Tobin had dashed off to make his way back to the shuttle. He thought to himself if he could get back to Nostalgia Dent could fix the mess up Tobin made. No one was going to be happy with this outcome he thought. When Tobin was walking by one of the lounge rooms he saw his uncle talking to a very pretty red head. Tobin stopped to watch, he never seen his uncle flirt before. The lady looked over her shoulder and stopped talking. To what Tobin thought to be a miracle his parents walked up and greeted his uncle and the lady. The red head shook their hands, gave his uncle a kiss, and left. Was he dreaming Tobin thought; this must be a trick Dent did somehow. Tobin seen his mother was pregnant it must be him as a baby in his mother's stomach. This would be his chance to change things for his family, he wouldn't lose his parents. Tobin walked into the lounge and went to go up to his parents, he was going to warn them and save their lives. Out of no ware he was jerked back and almost fell till he caught himself. Tobin turned to see it was the chief of the station Fauna; she came from a planet having a race of people who physically did not show their age. She looked the same to him as from his own time.

Fauna in a stern voice said "Tobin how did you get here?"

Tobin being scared said "Nostalgia's shuttle. How do you know my name?"

"I keep track of the time drift to see if it will affect the Gallant."

"You're with the T.W.C.?"

"Well, yes." Fauna stated sheepishly.

Tobin heard his mom say "Fauna congratulations, I heard you got chief lab technician."

Tobin new from the time period he came from Sarah held that position. Fauna replied "Thank you. "

Tobin's mother Mae said "Oh what a cute boy what's your name?"

Tobin responded "Tobin ma'am."

Fauna interjected "It's nice to see you Mae, Stan, and Edward, but Tobin here has a special task to attend to."

Tobin added "Hmm, right."

Mae finished with saying "I'll see you later."

Fauna in a hurry said "OK, bye." Then she looked at Tobin and said "Let's go."

Tobin nodded and followed her to her office. The office was simple and tidy looking; Fauna gestured for Tobin to sit down. Tobin sat and looked at her wondering what was going to happen. Fauna started by saying "What do you think you're doing, and how did you get the shuttle?"

Tobin answered "I was working for Dent on Nostalgia and I took the shuttle without him knowing."

"Why would you do that to Dent? He is going to have to answer for the repercussions of your actions." Fauna said in a stern tone.

Tobin panicked, stuttering, "I just wanted to go someplace I liked that I didn't have to leave. When I saw my mother and father I thought we could be together again as a family."

"You can't it would undo everything your parents ever did. It's unfair to tell you I can't allow you to change your parent's future. You must know that all the pain you have gone through has been a result of other lives being saved." Fauna said, trying to keep a firm tone.

"My parents built stations and did research they weren't doctors!" retorted Tobin.

"Your parents did a lot of heroic acts they never told anyone about. Your uncle doesn't even know what they really were doing. Of course they did build stations but fate brought them other opportunities to help people. And to change their course now would change so many other people's lives." Fauna stated as she rose from her chair.

"So? Not a big deal they wouldn't get the job they wanted or maybe wear a different suit that day. I don't think my parents left that much of an impacted on any one but me. I was the one they kept boarding off with relatives." Tobin fumed.

"Do you remember the mission they were on before they left for their very last mission? And how they came back late?" Fauna inquired.

"Yes."

"They had used their ship as a blockade to stop pirates from over running a supply ship with refugees on it."

"You're lying my dad doesn't have a heroic bone in his body. How do I know you're not messing with my head?" Tobin barked at her.

"Tobin I'm the chief of the Gallant if I were going to do anything to you. Do you think you would be standing here right now? I can mess with you anytime I want." Fauna said firmly.

"I can mess with you anytime I want." Tobin snapped back mockingly.

Fauna sat for some time not saying anything and just looked at him. Tobin thought she bought it she must be afraid of him. He wondered about her "Have I said that before to her, she looks as if I have?"

Tobin then said "What could you do; you can't hurt me you have to keep time save and me?"

"Double your home work load when I get you back to your own time. Tobin think you're here for a reason don't be selfish."

"I'll never be with my family again." Tobin grumbled to himself.

"You don't know that and you are with family. Your uncle cares about you." Fauna reassured him.

"I know that is why I wanted to leave. I don't want him hurt because of me. Anything I love always leaves; someway or somehow!" Tobin murmured.

"It's not your fault and it's not always going to be that way. Tobin look at me remember me, my face, and know I will be watching your path in life." Fauna said, locking eyes with Tobin.

"Watch me do what?" Tobin asked timidly.

"You are far too young to stay out of your own time line; and I can see Dent has pushed that limit. I need to get you back to your own time line very soon. You have to trust and believe me right now and I can answer your questions later." Fauna stated.

"Can I say good bye to my parents?" Tobin asked.

"No, their ship will be departing soon and so will you. You can watch them from the bay window the last thing I need is you having contact with yourself." Fauna said, still holding eye contact.

Tobin nodded his head. It felt like a long walk down to the bay. Tobin felt happy to see his parents but watching them load up into the shuttle like so many times before he could feel the pain grow. It was hard choking back the tears knowing it was his last time to see them. Fauna walked Tobin into the bay and over to Nostalgia's shuttle. She went into the cock pit with him, looked at the panel, and readjusted the settings. She began to talk to Tobin saying "You must be the smartest and bravest youngster I have ever met. How did you go about programming the shuttle?"

Tobin answered "I used a manual Marduc gave me."

"Not surprised. You see time travel is like baking cookies, change the recipe a little you'll get hard or soft cookies. If you put less of one ingredient you need to alter the other ingredients also. So you just don't alter your destination you change your speed as well. The thrusters are pressure sensitive so if you hit your destination without the right injection rate you miss the year you need all together."

"So why are you telling me this."

"I'll be setting you up to arrive just after you left Nostalgia. You still have to make sure you get there in case something happens. I can't just chase you around in time. I have other places to be to, understand?"

"Yes." Tobin nodded.

"When you get back to Nostalgia, I'll have Dent send you to the right time at the Gallant you need to be at."

"Can I say good bye to Dent?"

"Yes, and I'll have a talk with you. I'll then see what to do with you."

Fauna finalized the program settings. Before she left the shuttle she told Tobin "You have a great future don't miss it."

After that all Tobin had to do was sit back and let the shuttle do the navigating. Tobin picked up Jessy looked at him and started talking to him. "I guess we're not starting a new life somewhere else. We'll just be going back to our old one. You think Fauna is going to watch us all the time from now on? She is supposed to watch time not us, unless we are real time travelers. I wonder what will be in store for us."

Stan

Chapter 6

Hard Lesson

The trip back to Nostalgia was much smoother and faster than his trip from Nostalgia. When the shuttle landed in the bay Dent was there to meet him. Dent came up to him and began to speak with a tone of disappointment. "Tobin I was on my way to get you from your quarters for a celebration that had just started. We all were happy with the success we had with the store we felt a party was the best way to show it. Fauna messaged me before I could find you and told me I would find you here. I gathered the rest of your things, no sense in leaving the bay. It will be easier for me to take you back myself."

Tobin spoke up "I'm sorry. I didn't mean for it to be like this."

"You've done enough, in you go." Dent said in a firm manner.

Tobin seated himself in the back of the shuttle by the cargo hold. Dent went to the cockpit and started their voyage to the Gallant. By this time Tobin had his head buried in his arms. He couldn't handle another shuttle trip Tobin just wanted to get out and move around. During the trip Dent only said one statement being "I guess it wasn't the best idea to have you work for me after all."

The words cut deep to Tobin, the first time he made friends and he betrayed them. It's not like he meant to, he knew he would have to leave them anyway. When they arrived at the Gallant Fauna was there waiting for them. Dent escorted Tobin out of the shuttle and to Fauna. This time as the chief of the Gallant, Fauna started on Dent "Dent you should not have endangered Tobin. I should have not allowed for him to work for you. Your negligence will no doubt have your license suspended."

Dent humbly said "I apologize; I didn't have the foresight of these events. Tobin came to no harm, I'm sure he learned a great lesson from all this."

Fauna skeptically said "The only thing he learned was how to meddle with time. Tobin, give your pet over to Dent and go to your uncle."

Tobin stubbornly said "No! "

Fauna angered stated "Tobin…"

Tobin went on to say "This isn't Dents fault you have no right to punish him. He knows more about what people need and when they need it then you do. I need to have him for a friend and he needs to keep his store."

Dent humbled said "Tobin thank you and I think you should keep Jessy. After all I don't think anyone here will take the time to listen to you when you need it."

Fauna exasperated spoke "Fine you can keep your pet your uncle can deal with it. I'm still looking into what to do about you, Dent. Marduc is running interference to keep me out of your business; but your luck won't last.

You can leave for now but I will be in further contact with you about this."

Dent nodded "So it seems. Tobin." He motioned to the boy to approach.

Tobin came up to Dent; Dent knelt down and found two arms wrapped around him. Dent gave a light embrace, Tobin let go. Dent looked into his eyes and said "It was fun, wasn't it?"

Tobin "Yes."

Dent "You've grown more then what you think or look."

Dent got up, walked to the shuttle, looked back, and smiled before climbing into the shuttle to leave. Tobin didn't want to believe it was over or that he was back on the Gallant to stay. Fauna helped gather up Tobin's bag as he carried Jessy, and walked him to his uncle's quarters. Stan greeted them with a smile and asked how Tobin was.

Tobin answered "Good."

Stan continued with "Did they work you hard?"

"Yes."

Fauna interjected "It was good of you to let him go. I'll be doing a follow up with him later this week. It will be just a formality of course."

Stan acknowledged Fauna "OK, I'm sure everything will be fine."

Fauna looking at Tobin and spoke "I'll let you settle in and don't forget normal lessons start at the beginning of the new week."

Stan, with an air of euphoria about him said "I'm sure Tobin will love to get back to a normal routine."

Fauna went on her way and Stan scooted Tobin into their quarters. Stan looked at Tobin and said "It was hard for me to let you go for the trip, not knowing if you were coming back. I mean to say if anything were to happen to you. I think I can say I see life from your eyes now."

Just then Jessy wiggled and popped out of his bag. Stan smiled "Oh, I see you brought home a friend with you. What's his name?"

Tobin answered "Jessy. I'm happy to see you uncle."

Stan nodded, smiling said "I know and look at you. You must have hit a growth spurt."

Tobin "Yeah, I did didn't I."

Stan chuckled "Go unpack and settle in, I'll get dinner going."

Tobin felt happy and sad at the same time. Tobin looked at Jessy and said "At least I still have you." After dinner Tobin sat on his bed trying to put everything together in his head. It took him a bit to realize he had been up for thirty-two hours or a least that's what he figured it was. Time travel really messed with his sense of being. It was a lot to take in for Tobin and to understand everything that had happened. Seeing his parents and working on Nostalgia. Then being thrust back into an everyday life with his uncle. It was almost too much; at least he has the time now to reflect Tobin thought. He was soon asleep and then up in what he thought were minutes. This was because his uncle telling him good morning and to get up.

Stan took the day off to spend with Tobin; they started with a big full breakfast. Then they went to the recreation lobby to play games. After that they picked up some toys for Jessy. During lunch Tobin asked if his uncle ever had a girlfriend.

Stan replied "That is a strange question coming from you, are you starting to like girls?"

Tobin shyly said "No, I just wanted to know more about you and the life you lived."

Stan grinned sheepishly and replied "Okay then where to begin. I was a ladies man at one time. Girls would fawn over me quite a bit as I never stayed in a long term relationship. I only fell in love once, her name was Laura and she had a sister named Chrissy. It breaks my heart to think of her, she and her sister were on the same ship that your parents were on."

Tobin interrupted with "What did Chrissy look like?" He was curious was she the same Chrissy from Nostalgia.

Stan reminisced "She was a very nice looker too, a good person; she would always look out for her sister. Even gave me a hard time when I was dating Laura."

Tobin was stunned "I didn't realize how much the research ship being lost affected you. I only thought of myself and my parents, but never how much you lost as well."

Stan snapped back to the here and now "Never mind, let's not be talking about that anymore. I'm just happy to have you in my life. I get to play an important role in helping you become a man. Now let's take you and your little friend down to the green house to play."

Tobin agreed "I think Jessy would like that."

Tobin spent the rest of the day playing with Jessy and listening to music with his uncle. Somehow Tobin was feeling rewarded, but why he hadn't done anything good. In fact he did more harm this last week. Was it OK for him to be happy, Tobin thought? Towards the end of the day Stan took Tobin back to their quarters. When they got there he upgraded and added new programs to Tobin's holo computer. It was nice Tobin finally got a new set of games to play. Instead of playing the games Tobin decided to snuggle into bed. Lying in bed with his eyes closed Tobin heard a soft voice calling his name. He got up to look to see if someone actually was there. He sat up and saw Chrissy there looking at him. Tobin blurted out "What are you doing here?"

Chrissy answered "I never got a chance to say my good bye."

Tobin stammered "Chrissy how did you get in my room?"

Chrissy in sing song tone replied "I have my ways."

Tobin had to ask "Do you know my uncle; do you have a sister named Laura?"

Chrissy confirmed his suspicions "Yes, you must know I was on the Rochelle."

Tobin excitedly asked "Do you know where my parents are or can you help me find them?"

Chrissy tried her best to clarify "Slow down

I'll do my best to explain what happen. The Rochelle entered a freak time storm as the crew left for a contract mission. The first time a storm like that had happened; it's what caused the rift that is around Nostalgia. I do see your parents from time to time; everyone is still alive. The crew and passengers don't realize they are in a time paradox or mini-universe; they all think there at Nostalgia for repairs. You see their not far away we just have to find a way to bring everyone back."

Tobin looked at Chrissy with a determined face and said "I'll find a way to bring them all back and you too."

Chrissy replied "You're just a little boy."

Tobin, with a sense of purpose "I have a whole life ahead of me, I won't be little forever."

Chrissy smiled back at Tobin "We'll work together to bring them back."

Tobin implored "Can you tell my parents I love them and Laura that my uncle is still in love with her?"

Chrissy nodded "Yes, when I see them, the rift is very unpredictable. I'll have to go for now."

And with that said she gave Tobin a hug then vanished in to another time. Tobin was dumbfounded by what she had said. He couldn't close his eyes even though he tried; knowing that he had to master time to get his parents back.

Fauna

Chapter 7

New Clothes

The next week was fast paced for Tobin; he didn't try to make friends with the other children. Not like he didn't want to; he wasn't jaded towards them any more for having families. Tobin just was too busy locating the information and programs he needed about the theories and paradoxes of time travel.

At the weeks end Fauna sent for Tobin to come to her office. Tobin went not sure what to expect, he opened the door to see Fauna sitting behind a big desk reviewing logs.

She looked up and said "Tobin, so glad to see you came. Have a seat."

Tobin sat and replied "Is this where you give me my punishment?"

Fauna "No, it seems I've been told to watch you and not to interfere with what you are doing. I'm to guide you from undo able events."

Tobin bluntly asked "Fauna, if you know all about time? Why don't you go and bring back the Rochelle?"

Fauna looking back at her logs replied "It's not

my place to."

"Help me bring them back." Tobin pleaded.

Fauna looked up at Tobin "I can't, but others will."

Tobin "If you won't help me. I'm done talking." Tobin stood up and was going to leave when Fauna said "You should know when your next break from schooling comes you'll be spending it working on Nostalgia."

Tobin stopped turned around and said "You're going to letting Dent keep running his shop?"

Fauna continued "Marduc has seen to the store staying open. Truth is yours and Nostalgia's futures are intertwined. I can't stop you from going there if Dent will have you."

Tobin looked Fauna in the eyes firmly "Send him a message I will be there to make things right."

Tobin opened the door to see his uncle ready to come in. Stan smiled and said "You getting a talking to also?"

Tobin "You could say so; I'll be going back to our quarters."

Stan chuckled "Okay, I'll see you later."

Once it was just Stan and Fauna in the room. Fauna asked "What do you think about Tobin since he has been back from Nostalgia? Was it good for him to go?"

Stan thought upon the question "I missed him, but he did come back as a better person. We are on talking terms and getting along, big improvements."

Fauna brought up a report "You know I have gotten some complaints from the engineering department. It seems Tobin has been getting under their feet latcly."

Stan read the complaints "I do apologize for that. I think Tobin is trying to learn how to fix or build something. I don't know what it is."

Fauna closed the report "Well then, let us not discourage him. What do you think about Tobin going for another work release?"

Stan pondered for a moment "I'm OK with it; it will be good for him." With that said Stan left Fauna's presence and returned to his quarters.

It was late afternoon and Tobin was in his room using his holo computer. Stan knocked and then opened the door. Tobin looked at him and said "I guess you can come in."

Stan replied "You're never up to anything I can bust you on. I had a talk with your educators again."

Tobin scoffed "What did they say that I cheated."

Stan "No, the activities instructor said other children think you are creepy. And your teacher said you handed in lessons for next term; they want to put you in private lessons."

Tobin shrugged "That's fine with me."

Stan worried asked "Are you even trying to make friends?"

Tobin glanced at his uncle "I did try; the other children don't have anything in common with me. They just like it when I let them play with Jessy."

Stan sighed "I'll let them know to start you solo next term. What is that box thing you've been working on?"

Tobin grinned at his uncle "This little box is supposed to be an inner matter machine. I made it to store big items in a smaller space; I tried it on my pants."

Stan looked at Tobin in disbelief "So that's why I had to throw out half your laundry."

Tobin blinked and nodded "I'm Sorry, about that. I haven't worked out the bugs yet."

Stan gave the device a quick look over "If you get it working and plan on using it you might want to add a handle to it. Just as well, you are growing quick and I have to get you new clothes by the end of the week. Don't put anymore items in that thing use a real bag for your trip."

Tobin laughed "OK, I'll find something else to put into it."

Stan smirked at Tobin "Not Jessy."

Tobin laughed "Of course not Jessy. Did you get me the new programs?"

Stan rubbed his temple "Yes, you study too hard. I'm making you take the rest of the week off from studies to have fun. You'll need it I'm sure Dent will make you work hard and earn some muscles."

Tobin smiled at his Uncle "You're right."

Stan dumbfounded replied "I am?"

Amazing how a little time away had turned Tobin's life for the better Stan thought as he exited the room.

Early the next day Stan and Tobin started their activities. They ate a quick breakfast and were off to the garment lobbies to find Tobin better fitting outfits. Tobin was looking at the darker looking outfits when a red headed boy walked up and said "You're weird."

Tobin replied "So?"

The boy mockingly asked "What do you think you're doing?"

Tobin replied without even turning around "I'm getting outfits for a trip."

The boy retorted "A trip where, to the recycle room?"

Tobin glanced over his shoulder and replied "Nice idea, but I'm going to Nostalgia."

The boy stood there, arms crossed "That old dump of a station?"

Tobin slightly angered retorted "Its fine that you think that. But I'd rather be there, where I can eat what I want. I can go to sleep when I want, and meet knew interesting people who have been to more places then you'll ever see. So, you can stay here with your eight o'clock bed time. Dietary planned meals and listen to the event instructor tell you what to do."

The boy huffed "You're stupid."

After saying that the boy stomped off to find is mother. The boy didn't bother Tobin one bit. If it took being different and to be an outcast to get his parents back he would do it. The reward he will get is much bigger and more important than any teasing he suffered at the hands of the other children. Tobin went onto get outfits that were closer to adult work clothes. Basic yet functional is what he needed. When Stan and Tobin settled in their quarters they received a message for Tobin to meet Fauna early the next day. Tobin knew it was about the work trip no doubt. They did their usual night routine and afterwards Tobin spent a good chunk of the night fiddling with scraps of parts he found earlier.

Come morning Tobin had no delay meeting up with Fauna, he had questions of his own for her. Fauna was just going over her tasks for the day when Tobin entered the office. "Ah! Good morning Tobin." Fauna said when she seen him.

Tobin replied "Good morning ma'am."

Fauna smiled "You're doing well I see. I received the request for the programs you asked for. I decided they were not going to be a good fit for you. I'm going to upgrade you to a more advanced program to suit your needs."

Tobin astounded said "Thank you, I would like to ask something of you."

Fauna rose an eyebrow at Tobin "You think your privileged enough to ask favors of me?"

Tobin stated "It would keep me out of the lab and your hair."

Fauna nodded "I'm listening, proceed."

Tobin cleared his throat and asked "Is the extended storage room in the recycle center being used and if not can I use it?"

Fauna paused for a moment "Our station does its best not to keep junk around so of course it is empty. I'm sure your thinking of stashing broken junk parts in there."

Tobin stammered "It's not exactly junk at least not when I'm done with it."

Fauna nodded at Tobin "You can have the room just don't do anything too outlandish. I'm sure the rest of the staff will be delighted to hear you'll be leaving them alone for a change."

Tobin smiled "That helps me so much."

Fauna wistfully asked "Are you ready to go back to Nostalgia?"

Tobin nodded as he replied "Yes, all prepared."

Fauna made eye contact with Tobin "This time it is going to have to be a shorter visit, but you will go more often over there. This is so that your growth spurts can be better explained to others. Understand?"

Tobin smiled "Yes, I would like it that way; it would let me see my uncle more often. You don't think that Dent is going to still be upset with me do you?"

Fauna was surprised by Tobin's statement and replied "I'm sure he wasn't upset with you in the beginning of all this. He didn't start out as a pro time traveler; he had a lot of help from others."

Tobin was relieved "That helps I feel better about

going now."

Fauna motioned with her hand "Off with you, I have work to do and you should try not to be so serious. Take a break for the day."

Tobin replied "OK."

And with that said Tobin was on his way to the lobbies viewing room. Every year about this time for a good week the Planet Alpha Phoenix has a pretty purple hue to it. It is caused by particles in the atmosphere nothing magical to it but yet it seemed so. It is the closest planet to the Gallant and nice to watch when you have the time to. Tobin arrived to see others doing as he thought to do, no bother still plenty of room to see out the viewing port. Tobin found a nice spot to view the planet; this was one of his favorite things to do. It always made him feel at peace, Tobin looked over the other people that were there and one stuck out rather oddly. A short man in his forties with red hair, full beard, and strangely dressed. Tobin wasn't one to talk to unfamiliar people, but he couldn't stop himself from approaching the man.

Tobin walked over to the man and began talking to him by saying "Pardon me sir but I don't ever recall seeing you here before. Are you visiting?"

The man looked at Tobin, wrinkled his nose and answered "I visit once a year. Is there a reason you need to know?"

Tobin flustered said "Sorry, curiosity got the better of me. You just look like you belong somewhere else. Have you ever been to Nostalgia?"

The man cocked his head "Why yes, it is a good

place to find things."

Tobin felt relieved "I thought as much, I've been doing work over there and I thought I might have seen you."

The man scratched his beard "I don't remember seeing you there. My name is David Beacon. You can call me Dave and your name?"

Tobin promptly replied "Tobin Guide it's an honor to make your acquaintance."

Dave stated with a grin "Yes, it is."

Tobin overflowing with curiosity continued his talk "How far do you come to watch the planet every year?"

David looked back at Tobin and replied "Pretty far, I live on planet Forge. It is a planet of industrial factories."

Tobin stated "I read about it in Dents logs. A lot of the station's parts came from there."

David nodded at Tobin "You must have access to great knowledge."

Tobin thought over what David had said and answered "Some but I still need to learn more."

David scratched his beard once more "I should be on my way, perhaps I'll see you again."

Tobin smiled "It would be nice, and then I could get to know you better."

David outstretched his hand "Perhaps on Nostalgia we'll meet again."

David shook Tobin's hand and left to go down the hall. Tobin thought it all rather odd maybe there paths are meant to meet. Tobin stayed a little longer to watch the planet's beauty; he took Jessy out of his bag from where the little one was sleeping. Jessy seemed to like the colors fading in and out as much as Tobin did. Tobin looked at Jessy and said "Well, little guy let's go back and meet up with Uncle Stan. I'm sure it's time to get some dinner."

Tobin slipped Jessy back into his bag and headed back to his quarters. When there he seen his uncle had the same mind set and was already preparing the meal. Stan looked to see Tobin enter and started talking toward him "It's our last night together. At least this leave will be shorter; this place does feel lonesome without you. I'll make sure you eat well tonight."

Tobin responded "It's okay, dinner will turn out great and I'll be just fine."

Stan deep down didn't want Tobin to leave, but he knew it was good for him. The last trip helped Tobin come out of his shell. Stan was sure more visits to Nostalgia would bring out the best in Tobin. After their dinner Stan helped Tobin get all his clothes and items he need up and gathered around. When Tobin was packed he loaded and looked at some of his new programs. They were loaded with physics, math, and science. Just what he needs to get a handle on the theories he had been asking about. When he was done he told his uncle good night and then tucked Jessy and himself into bed. Tobin was looking forward to the next day, but didn't know what to expect.

Chapter 8

Some Changes

It was early in the morning and Tobin was already in the docking bay. This time his uncle was there to send him off, the two of them got up early and had a quick breakfast to spend some extra time together. Stan was happy to be there to send Tobin off and even started to be envious of the time Tobin got to spend off the station. Tobin didn't talk much about what he did over on Nostalgia but Stan was starting to think it must be pretty interesting to keep Tobin coming back.

It wasn't long before the shuttle from Nostalgia showed up; after docking Marduc exited the shuttle with a warm smile on his face. Tobin was happy it was Marduc that came to bring him to the station. It had been a long time since he seen him last. He was dressed similar to what David was wearing when Tobin had met him, interesting Tobin thought. Marduc came up to meet Tobin and Stan with a handshake.

Marduc said to Stan "Your nephew here seems to be a good worker, to have Dent request to have him back at Nostalgia and that is a privilege."

Stan responded "I always have good faith in him."

Marduc turned to Tobin and said "You already to go Tobin."

Tobin answered with "Hmm. Yes Sir."

Tobin went to go grab for his bags and Jessy when Stan stopped him and gave him a big hug. Stan said sheepishly "I couldn't help myself it's going to be a while before I can pick on you."

Tobin responded with "The professor of science going soft on me."

Stan stated proudly "You're becoming good in the field yourself."

Marduc interjected with a state of urgency "This is all heartwarming. But I came here to take you to Nostalgia and we best be going."

With that said Tobin with the help of Marduc gathered up his bags and loaded them up with themselves in to the shuttle. Stan made sure to watch them leave from the elevator lift. In the shuttle Tobin made sure to sit up in the cockpit across from Marduc so as to watch him pilot the shuttle.

Marduc looked over towards Tobin and said "You ought to know there has been changes since you have last been to Nostalgia."

Tobin was panicked "Have they been big changes? Like things being moved around or is the shop still there? Dent didn't close it, did he?"

Marduc shook his head no "The shop is still open. There have been some changes to appearances though."

Tobin sighed in relief "Looks different, I'm sure it

can't be too bad."

Marduc looked from the console to Tobin "Truthfully I'm surprised you're coming back. You and Dent are both stubborn; it's hard to believe the two of you get a long."

Tobin sternly stated "Dent is a smart man. I'd be happy to be like him."

Marduc turned back to console as he adjusted the controls. "Genius yes he is, but I don't know if you should be just like him alas. You Tobin have the ability to do so much more."

Tobin was pleased with this and replied "It would take a lot of doing and I have a lot yet to do. For now I'll have to look up to him and you. I'll just try my best."

Marduc grinned at what he heard "Good kid."

It wasn't long before they were docked at Nostalgia and left the shuttle. Tobin looked around; they were at the older shuttle bay. He then said "I thought we would have been greeted does Dent not cares to see us this time?"

Marduc answered "Not the case he just is wrapped up in what he is doing at the moment. Let's go and put your bags in your quarters. Dent is going to want you to start working right away. This place has been all out of sorts. Things are out of place and they require your special touch."

Tobin nodded in agreement "I guess I better start right away then."

And with that they were onto the tasks of getting Tobin's things settled in. Tobin then gathered Jessy up into his bag and with Marduc went to take the elevator to the shop. Tobin was feeling happy with himself being able to be back and so needed. The elevator was its usual efficiency with a short moment Tobin was peering over the shop. It didn't appear to be out of too much disarray since he last seen it, which made him think Marduc was elaborating on the condition of the shop. Tobin came into the shop with Marduc expecting to see Dent. Instead of Dent he saw a handsome younger looking man standing behind the counter with Chrissy.

The man looked at Tobin and said to him "You must be the little fellow I was told would come."

Tobin perplexed said "Pardon?"

The man frantically rustled through his papers and electronic logs "It's here in my notes that I left myself. It says you would be a great help to me. We haven't properly introduced ourselves yet, I'm Dent. And you are?" The man paused and then said "Your named was deleted from the log when it malfunctioned."

Tobin cautiously stated "Tobin."

Dent's eyes twinkled "I knew a great man with the name Tobin. He helped make me what I am today."

With a wink and smile Chrissy added to the conversation "Great men start in little packages."

Dent looked to Chrissy with confusion "They start as little boys; where did you learn anatomy from? I left instructions in my notes on what needs to be done. No time for long intro's, there is plenty to be done."

Tobin thought this is what was mentioned by changes to appearances, so that person before him should be the same Dent.

Tobin asked trying to asset the situation "Are you Dent's son?"

Dent answered a bow of the head "You must be confused, this has nothing to do with my father. I am the do it all, find it all time traveler Dent. If you needed it I have it, will find it, or you don't need it. That is who I am and what I do."

Tobin was confused "So you are no relation to the prior owner of this shop?"

Dent raised an eyebrow "I've always have been the owner of this shop, I had it set up." Dent paused, put his index finger up to his lips, and took a deep breath. He then looked in tensely at Tobin and began to explain "All right, this is how it worked out. You see I thought having an antique shop would be the thing for me; I so love old things. Which was a great idea except it would take a lot of time to do. So, I decided I would put it off until I was older when I knew I 'had plenty of time to do it. Now that I know I have it set up; like I wanted I can enjoy running it without all the extra work. The only thing is I eventually do have to go out and find all the items for the shop, but that can wait. Does that explain everything for you?"

Tobin thought it over "Yes, it does sir. The "you" I know is older and wiser."

Dent cocked his head to one side "What was meant by that?"

Tobin shook his head "It was nothing. You just must be very clever to make all this happen."

Dent smiled at what Tobin had said "You're right I am rather clever, so let's say we get some work done."

Tobin grumbled "We should; this place needs it."

Chrissy added "You came back to us feisty, now come with me I'll get you started."

With that Marduc took his leave of the group as Chrissy walked Tobin over to one of the corner racks were there was a stack of boxes. She began saying "This looks like a good spot to get started. It's okay to be thrown off; the rest of us are still adjusting to the changes. Dent has Trace's orders and schedules all messed up, it will be a while before things are straightened up."

Tobin asked fearfully "Did this happen because of me?"

Chrissy looked him in the eyes "Oh no, he doesn't even know anything that happen when you were here last. Don't worry about it; with you here we'll have everything put back into order, and the shop up and running in a few days."

Tobin felt better "Then there is no doubt in my mind I should be here helping."

Chrissy whispered to Tobin "There are some other things for me to show and tell you, later on of course."

Tobin whispered back "Really?"

Dent from the other side of the room hollered at them "I hear a lot of talking over there. You two had best be having a lot of work being done with that chatter."

Chrissy shouted back "Don't worry it will get done." Dent just stood at the counter mumbling to him as he shuffled through more notes and logs. Chrissy looked at Tobin and said in a low voice "He is going out of his way to be a pain."

Tobin said "We'll have to give him a chance. Let's get this work done then I'm sure he'll be his old happy self"

Chrissy looked back at Tobin with a grin, "It'll be a long time before that."

Tobin smiled and nodded his head, for the rest of the day they were quietly hard at work. Dent did quite a lot of checking in on them. Tobin thought he was trying to figure out why his other self-left him with the staff he now has. It was early evening when Chrissy and Tobin finished the boxes they had worked out of. The two of them were on their way to the cafeteria, when Dent stopped them before they could get on the elevator.

Dent inquired of them "Are you two done? You need to check in with me on your progress before you leave."

Chrissy stammered "Sorry didn't think to; you have never had us do that before."

Dent looked at them in disbelief, "And how am I to know that is true?"

Chrissy sighed "You picked us; you put it into your notes and had faith in us to work for you again."

Dent seemed appeased by this answer, "I suppose you're justified in your reasoning, but from here out you need to be checking in with me more often and before you leave."

Tobin added to the conversation saying "You plan on staying in the shop more?"

Dent was baffled "Of course haven't I always? This is my shop and it is where I should be."

Chrissy stated "You used to spend a lot of time in shipping."

Dent furrowed his brow "I don't think there is anything there that would keep me long."

Chrissy rolled her eyes "If you say so. Come Tobin let's get some dinner."

Tobin looked at Jessy and Said "Come Jessy let's get some dinner."

Jessy's ears perked and snapped to attention and came to Tobin.

Chrissy and Tobin giggled and then got into the elevator, leaving Dent to himself. Chrissy picked out a very nice dinner for the two of them when they arrived at the cafeteria. They didn't wait long for their food to be served, and were able to start enjoying the delicious meal. Part way through the meal Chrissy started conversation with Tobin saying" I've been snooping around and found the most wonderful thing for you."

Tobin excitedly asked "You did, is it good?"

Chrissy smiled and leaned in close and whispered "Yes."

Tobin's curiosity grew "Well, what is this mysterious thing?"

Chrissy continued "I found that one of the rooms on Nostalgia is a library."

Tobin was confused "Like a data bank? We have a

room for that on the Gallant."

Chrissy shook her head "No, it is similar to a data bank. The library is a room with books that you can read."

Tobin's face lit up "Like the old ones Dent has in shop."

Chrissy smiled "Right, there is something special about the library. It has books from all over the galaxy and there are books about time travel and theory of it. In a couple of days I'll take you there and you can start reading the books. They may help lead you to find a way to fix the time storm, and get your parents back."

Tobin had a thought "Speaking of the storm you seem to be more fixed here on Nostalgia."

Chrissy looked away from Tobin momentarily "For now I am, I haven't been shifted lately."

Tobin smiled and said "I like having you around."

Chrissy smiled and went back to eating her food. After eating Chrissy made sure Tobin got back to his quarters for the night and then retired herself to her quarters. Tobin started the next day early in hopes of having the work finished sooner to have the shop opened. He found Dent already in the shop looking over his notes and muttering under his breath. Tobin looked around and didn't see Chrissy, so he went to work on that day's project. He thought to himself as he was opening a box "It would have been hard to earn Dent's trust back after he had taken the shuttle. But this is a different Dent and he has just met me for the first time, or at least I think. And yet it seems harder to gain his trust compared to the other time they had met."

Tobin took Jessy out of his warm bag and let him play, Jessy never ventured far from Tobin. It was about an hours' time when Chrissy came to the shop. She head up to the desk to check in with the tasks Dent may have had for her. Tobin watched as Chrissy was talking to Dent, Dent seemed to get more frustrated. Tobin stopped working and walked up to the desk to see if there was something he could do to calm Dent.

When he got up to the counter he heard Dent saying "Why would I ever have Trill be my supplier?"

Chrissy responded by saying "She does your special orders, fills them and delivers them."

Dent was not amused "Not any more, we will not have any more special orders. Trace is just going to have to deal with all the orders and find other suppliers."

Dent threw his hands up in the air and turned his back to Chrissy.

Chrissy firmly placed her hands on the counter, "OK then, do you want me to tell Trace?"

Dent whipped back around "No, I need to get some things I'll do it on my way. As for you two, you better be fast to work when I get back." Dent grabbed a holo computer pad and briskly left the shop.

Tobin looked at Chrissy and said "What was that about?"

Chrissy answered "His special orders come from a woman whom used to time travel with him."

Tobin tried to comprehend "They have a falling out?"

Chrissy chuckled "You could say that, she got her own time machine and didn't need him. Dent didn't like the fact that she went solo."

Tobin in disbelief asked "How do you know all these things?"

Chrissy shrugged "I talk to customers, guests, and when Marduc is in the mood he'll tell me stories."

Tobin was pleased "That must be exciting to listen to. Have you met Trill?"

Chrissy in a rush, "Yes, she is nice and smart too. Enough talk let's get to work before Dent catches us." Chrissy and Tobin walked over to the boxes Tobin had been working on to find Jessy trying to make a bed out of a coat.

Tobin sighed then said "You little rascal come on out of there."

Chrissy added "Tobin I'll see what I can find we'll make him his own little bed out of one of the small boxes."

Tobin looked at Jessy as he picked him up and said "You'd like that, won't you?" Jessy did a chirp like noise to Tobin as to say yes. The two of them settled Jessy into his bed, and went straight to tagging and cataloging the items in the boxes. Dent came back some time later to the shop. He went about his business checking the list of items to be displayed. Tobin was determined to get the shop running soon, so he could get to the library on a day off. Tobin thought when the shop opened Dent would be too busy to bother with Chrissy and himself. Chrissy and Tobin were making good progress with their work when Dent came up to them and asked about a mini statue.

Chrissy answered him saying "It should be in that cabinet over there." Chrissy walked with Dent over to the cabinet to find the cabinet opened. Chrissy said to Dent "It's unlocked and the statue is missing but I know I left it locked."

Dent responded with "I had left it opened. I had more things to put in there, but I didn't see the statue."

Dent stood with his arms crossed as he spoke to Chrissy. His eyes darted back and forth between the empty cabinet and Chrissy's face.

Chrissy asked "Did you forget that the statue moves on its own? It's just like the big golem statue we have on display."

Dent ruffled his hair "Must have slipped my mind. Oh well. No harm done. I'm sure it will turn up later."

Chrissy shook her head "I'll be locking the case for right now, there are other items that do need to be left in there for safety. Please be mindful you did have the shop set up in a certain way for a reason."

Dent nodded "Your right, I'll have to keep with the pattern that's already set up."

Chrissy smirked "That's right."

Dent flustered changed the subject, "So, how is the sorting and tagging going?"

Chrissy looked over the current log "It's going well. We'll have everything ship shape by the end of the week."

Dent seemed pleased, "Yes, I see. I'll leave you to your work then."

Chrissy nodded and walked back over to Tobin as to help with the box. Chrissy started talking to Tobin as they worked "It will be a lot of work looking after him, I'm not always available for questions."

Tobin was alarmed, "You still phase out?"

Chrissy nodded, "Some but it is getting less."

Tobin inquired "Have you seen my parents lately?"

Chrissy eyes brightened "I'm still setting up something special for them. The answer is yes."

Tobin was baffled "Special; what do you mean?"

Chrissy pointed at Tobin "You'll find out later. And they are eager to see you again they still think they are waiting for ship repairs so they can complete the contract."

Tobin started to tear up, "I hope I can help to get them back."

Chrissy spoke softly, "I know you can do it, now if we can just get Dent to help without him knowing."

Tobin rubbed his eyes "He would not like us to try?"

Chrissy explained "He's the kind of person who thinks things should be best if left alone and if you try to change them it would make things worse for everyone. Also I'm sure he would frown on a ten year old trying to alter time or events."

Tobin thought it over, "Good reasoning; it will be up to us to fix things."

Chrissy and Tobin worked hard tagging and placing items in the shop until it was in the late evening. They began to pick up empty boxes and put away trash when Dent came up to them. He began saying "I see you two decided to work late. The two of you are moving pretty quickly through those boxes, I think we'll be in fine shape."

Chrissy beamed "That's because you have the best little guy on the job."

Tobin smiled and Dent continued to prattle on "He is a studious worker, maybe I did line up good help for myself after all."

With that said Dent decided to leave for the night. Tobin and Chrissy finished up for the night, gathered up Jessy, and went to eat. After dinner the two of them went their separate ways.

Chapter 9

The Library

Tobin was tired so he grabbed up Jessy, put his bag up, and went to bed. He was sleeping sound when a crash woke him up. Tobin pushed himself up and looked around the room to see what had happened. He found that it was a cup he had left on the table that was knocked over. Tobin thought Jessy must have done it looking for some water to drink. Tobin went and filled his dish thinking that would take care of the issue. He picked up the glass and scolded Jessy for making the mess. When Tobin went to go back to his room he found the statue Dent was looking for. He thought it was odd but by now he learned not to question things on the station. They will just occur for the sake of being there. He set the figure up on the table and was going to get it back to the shop in the morning. Tobin had just gotten to his room when he heard shuffling in the main room. He turned back to look and see what it was. The figure was out of sight, this is to be expected Tobin thought. How was he going to get Dent the figure?

Tobin turned to Jessy and said he was sorry and patted him on the head. He realized it must have been the figure moving around that caused the cup to fall. He knew there was nothing he could do so he went back to bed. He rolled around trying to find his comfortable spot to sleep. Tobin then looked at the night stand and seen the figure staring back at him. Tobin sat up, what was he to do? He couldn't sleep with that thing looking at him all night. Was this going to be a stare down with a figure? Tobin poked it; the statue felt solid enough and didn't move. It was indeed a static item. Jessy jumped into Tobin's lap causing hair to fly into Tobin's nose making him sneeze at the statue. The figure began moving trying to wipe off the snot Tobin put on it. It was funny to watch a half man half goat figure prance around franticly trying to clean itself. Tobin giggled and the figure stopped, cocked its head, and with a puzzled look watched Tobin.

Tobin stopped and said "I'm sorry I didn't mean it."

The figure nodded showing Tobin it understood him. Tobin then said "You are a strange little thing aren't you."

Tobin patted it on the head and then opened his hand for good gesture. He then Said "See no harm done, I won't hurt you."

The figure climbed into his hand, Tobin moved it closer to get a better look at the figure. Even though the figure was made of wood, its fur seemed realistic. Tobin rubbed the figure on its back to pet it; the figure seemed to like it. The two of them were getting along rather well.

Tobin told it "I've got to get some sleep before the morning comes; Dent will have me working hard." The figure nodded, Tobin placed it on the stand where the figure solidified itself. Tobin curled into bed covering himself and stared at the figure until he fell asleep.

When Tobin woke in the morning and seen the figure was still on the stand. He picked it up, walked to the dining table, and sat it down on the table. He then proceeded to get ready for work. When Tobin was ready and had everything in order, he grabbed his bag and looked towards the figure. It was still sitting on the table. Tobin then looked at Jessy and said "Looks like you're going to have to share your bag today. Okay in you go." Tobin crouched down and Jessy climbed into the bag. Tobin stood up; resettled the bag around, and put the figure in too.

"Now we just got to manage to get to the shop. And try to find a way to explain to Dent everything." Tobin said to himself. After taking a deep breath he was out the door and on to the elevator lift. It paused long enough to open for Trace to get on. The next stop was the shop. When the elevator lift opened Dent was standing in the front of a rack of clothes pawing through it.

When he seen Trace and Tobin get off the lift he said "Have you two seen Chrissy anywhere?"

Tobin answered. "No."

Trace replied "You know she comes and goes."

Dent added "Oh that's right." Dent continued to rustle through the clothing; adding more disarray than productivity.

Tobin walked up to Dent and went on to tell him "I found the figurine statue you were looking for." Tobin grabbed it out of his bag and held it out to show Dent. Tobin went on to say "It must have found its way into my bag. The figure kept moving around in my quarters for most of the night."

Dent interjected "It's no good to me now. It seems

to have bonded with you. You might as well keep it; you can consider it payment for helping me."

Tobin relieved said "Thank you. I'm sure it will be helpful in some way."

Dent gave an awkward smile, "It looks like you are on your own today. I have your tasks set over there." Dent pointed to a stack of boxes and a pile of clothes he had thrown on the floor. Tobin put the figure in his bag, and went to sort out the mess that was left for him.

After Tobin walked away Trace said to Dent "I have your inventory list of all the supplies that have been ordered and delivered."

Dent responded. "Good. Have you found anyone to do our special orders?"

Trace "Umm. No. Most time travelers do not like to work to get items that they won't be keeping."

Dent "Yes, or they want a ransom for them. There must be a way around the problem. Keep working on it Trace."

Trace sighed, "OK."

Trace dismissed herself. Dent went back to looking through the rack; and muttered to himself "I wonder if that would look good on me?"

As Dent was looking Tobin wasted no time making order out of the mess Dent left him. For a while everything stayed quiet while Tobin worked, until he noticed the figure had moved itself from the bag. Tobin stopped what he was doing and said to the figure "If you're going to be out and about the least you can do is help with a little of the work." The figure walked over to the inventory scanner picked it up and solidified itself to act as a holder for it. Tobin remarked "That's using your head."

Throughout the day he would look up from his work to see Dent in different outfits. Tobin thought at least it was good he was wearing them and they were not on the floor. With the help of Jessy and Tobin's new friend the work was done sooner than they expected. Tobin went up to where Dent was fussing over shoes.

Tobin spoke loudly to get Dent's attention. "You should stick with the black pair."

Dent turned around to face Tobin and said "Oh, you think so? How are you coming along over there in your corner?"

Tobin smiled, "I think so. I'm finished. Is there anything I can work on to finish the day?"

Dent "No. You're done for the day and you can take the next two off. We have everything just about to my liking."

Tobin jokingly said, "OK. You're just going to fuss with everything till then. I suppose?"

Dent shot Tobin a stern look, "I don't fuss. I just need things to be right. After your two days off, the shop will be open again. So try and have some fun."

Tobin nodded in agreement, "OK. I will." Tobin went to gather his things, he grabbed the figure, Jessy, and was off to have dinner. As Tobin was arriving at the cafeteria, so was David the strange man he met on the Gallant.

David stopped, smiled, and then said "What a

surprise to see you again young man."

Tobin responded "Hello. I did mention I worked here on and off."

David "Oh that's right, you did. How about you join me for dinner then? I'll order us up some delights you wouldn't think possible."

Tobin jumped at the opportunity, "I have no prior engagements for dinner. I see no reason to reject the offer."

David motioned to a table, "We will dine of the food of my home planet. Let's be seated."

The dinner was as good as David promised and plenty was ordered to fill David's big appetite. David told Tobin great stories about his people and how they could forge and build anything. David then took Tobin for a walk through the station, were they could view Alpha Phoenix.

David stood starring at it with sadness in his eyes. He then said "Do you know what the planet was before it was uninhabitable?"

Tobin answered "No."

David "It was my ancestor's home, where my race of people came from."

Tobin wanted to know more, "What happened to it?"

David "They were tricked by merchants to use an oil on their crops to make them grow bigger and faster. They left quickly after they were paid. My people used the oil on the crops and it did as the merchants said it would. After they harvested the crops the soil started to put off a gas. The gas then poisoned our air, soil, and water causing them to leave their beautiful home."

Tobin's heart sank, "I see why you look sad. Is there anything that can be done to heal your home planet?"

David looked firmly at Alpha Phoenix and said "Yes, I believe there is. I have been working on a way to heal it using time travel. No one from my race believes it will work, so as a result I have had no help. I've been working and putting parts together to build a device to use. The only problem is I need at least one other person to help me operate it. Sadly I have not found anyone that would risk it all and join my cause."

Tobin looked at David and thought his cause was as true as his own. Tobin then said "If you can teach me about time travel I will in return find a way to help you heal your home planet."

David responded "You are about the right height. But how would you be able to do so being watched by so many other people. Dent surely would not approve of a young one doing these sorts of tasks."

Tobin looked at David "Hmm, Don't worry I have a work room on the Gallant to myself and I have access to discarded parts. No one would miss them and I do a work study on my own. So, I don't attend classes that would bog me down."

David stroked his beard and inquired "You would have to be back on the Gallant to help me."

Tobin with a smile replied "It should work out I will only be on Nostalgia two weeks at a time. So that no would notice any difference of my age."

David was intrigued "Why do you, want to learn time travel?"

Tobin looked to his feet as he replied "It's not that I want to time travel. I want to save my parents from the time storm they are caught in."

David nodded "Your cause is of honor. I will teach you in exchange for your help."

Tobin felt relieved "Thanks."

David stood up from the table "It is late, I will be leaving now and we will meet later when you're on the Gallant again."

Tobin agreed with David they shook hands and went their separate ways. Tobin retired to his quarters and went to sleep that night with great hope that he and David would have their happiness that they were seeking. Tobin started to wake up and was startled by Chrissy poking him in the side. Tobin rubbed his eyes and said "What was that for?"

Chrissy smiled and replied "Come on its time to get up and do things."

Tobin "It's early, Dent doesn't need me today."

Chrissy poked him again "You need to get up and going if you want to see what I have found for you."

Tobin got up and shooed Chrissy out so he could dress. After that he grabbed his bag, figure, and Jessy. And brought them with him to breakfast accompanied by Chrissy. During breakfast Chrissy was quiet but smug looking. Tobin couldn't take it any longer and blurted out

"What are you up to?"

Chrissy between bites said "We're going to go to the library I found. To see if we can find anything about time travel."

Tobin stopped mid bite "You could have told me sooner I would have skipped breakfast."

Chrissy giggled "No, it's more fun to tease you and make you wait."

Tobin sighed, and started eating quicker, and then dumped the rest of his food in the bag for Jessy. Tobin then said "Come on hurry up and eat your food."

Chrissy remarked "Coming from the boy who didn't want to get out of bed."

Tobin huffed "It's different now and who wants to be poked?"

Chrissy laughed and pushed the last of her food away and then said "Let's go. But be quite and walk softly."

Tobin remarked "Haven't left yet."

Chrissy shook her head and started to walk away. Tobin grabbed his bag and jumped out of his chair to join her. The two of them walk the halls in Nostalgia for what seemed for ever to Tobin. He watch as the walls changed from new chrome looking to old steel panels, and last they were aluminum in looks with dings and corrosion on them. Tobin thought how the station can hold together with all these different materials.

They came to a rusted heavy door and Chrissy stopped to say "We're here, let's go in." Chrissy opened the door as the hinges creaked and the room seemed to let forth a gasp. Tobin stopped and followed her into an expansive room with books, shelves, computer stations, and other electronic storage devices. The library had ladders going up to high selves. And the ceiling was a round dome if you let your eyes follow it down to the walls you would see they were painted to simulate a wooden pattern. It was as if Dent was trying to make it look like one he had seen in his travels. Tobin still couldn't understand the binding of information on paper and let alone the purpose of keeping them. Tobin walked right up to one of the computer pads and picked it up to see if it worked.

Chrissy watched him and said to Tobin "You should look at the books too."

As Tobin fiddled with the pad "Why they are outdated? I don't see why Dent keeps them around."

Chrissy answered with her hands on her hips "Because there are untested and never proven theories in them."

Tobin shrugged "I guess I'll be looking through them as well."

Chrissy gave Tobin a look of disbelief. She left Tobin to look through the data bases while she went through the books. Both Tobin and Chrissy grew discouraged with the task at hand. Tobin found that most the pads had no power or any way of charging them. The pads he managed to get running were in encrypted or about time travelers and not about actual time travel. Chrissy on the other hand was faced with books that were in languages she didn't understand. The two of them spent more time than they expected going through what the library had. Tobin and Chrissy were beginning to think they were not going to find anything useful to them, but as luck would have it they did find some useful notes hand written in a few of the books and one computer pad Tobin got working. He found one that he could understand the coding to and make for it to be readable to him. Chrissy and Tobin felt satisfied with what they had found. They gathered up the pad and books and took them to Tobin's quarters. Chrissy left Tobin and let him know she would be back the next day to check on his progress. Tobin snacked on some treats he had and looked through the books. They seemed simple enough to understand and when it came to looking at the pad, it seemed to almost be above Tobin's understanding. Tobin decided he would set it aside and ask David to help him with it. For now he was going to focus on reading the books and looking at the notes.

Chrissy

Chapter 10

Past Shadows

    Mae was watching out the viewing port as the Rochelle had passed the old space station Nostalgia. The Rochelle was medium sized freighter and soon be out of sight of the station. Nostalgia was a dying station, most of its crew had left and only a few remained to operate it. Mae was hesitant to leave for the trip she didn't like to have to leave her seven year old son Tobin. He was left with his uncle but it didn't make Mae feel any less of a bad parent for it. Mae and her husband Edward had signed contracts to set up stations for a company well before they found out they were going to be parents. The two of them only had to set up a couple more stations and then they could move on and give Tobin the family life he deserved. As Mae was in mid thought the ship began to rumble; they must have hit some turbulence. Alarms started to go off and lights began to flash. Mae lost her footing and found herself on the floor. It must be bigger then she thought could it be one of those freak storms they were having in that area. As quick as it came it was gone. The ship was silent and there was a mist about the ship. Had the life support been damaged? Mae heard a voice come over the intercom. It said "This is your captain speaking. The ship has taken damage. We are running on auxiliary power. I have changed our course to Nostalgia for repairs.

    Morning came and Tobin was sluggish. He looked at Jessy who had no intent on getting off the bed; Tobin left him in his little nest of covers. Tobin had a night with strange dreams he stretched and yawned and went to get water. He looked around and seen the figure on the table. He thought to himself "I need to come up with a name for the figure." As Tobin was pondering to himself Chrissy opened his quarter's door. Tobin looked at her and said "Do you believe in giving a person their privacy. You could have asked to be let in, what if I was dressing?"

    Chrissy responded with an eye roll "Don't be concerned. You're like a little brother to me."

    Tobin grumbled "Just a little warning would be nice."

    Chrissy giggled "Next time I'll scream to let you know I'm here."

    Tobin shot her a disapproving look "Thanks!"

    Chrissy motioned to Tobin "Come on lets go."

    Tobin shook his head "I don't get a day to myself."

    Chrissy teasingly said "If you do you would miss what you are going to see, and you will never forgive yourself."

    Tobin let out a sigh "OK, let me grab Jessy."

    Chrissy shook her head "Leave him, let him sleep. I need to just bring you with me to the lounge."

    Tobin seemed frustrated "Let's go. After the lounge we eat?"

Chrissy smiled "Yes."

It didn't take long for the two of them to get to the lounge. As they walked up to the opening, Tobin could see his parents setting in the lounge chairs. Before Tobin could get to them Chrissy stopped him. She then said "Your parents are in a temporal time flux pocket, it doesn't happen often and it is only here for a little bit of time. When we go in be careful and stay alert to your surroundings. I've told your parents your uncle brought you to them for a short visit. You understand? And don't tell them about the time storm."

Tobin didn't hold still when Chrissy took her hands off his Shoulders. Tobin said "Got it." He then dashed into the room to his parents. Upon seeing Tobin his parents stood up and embraced him into their arms. They went on to talk and spend time together. Tobin told his parents that he and his uncle were doing well and not to worry about them. His parents were happy to see Tobin and were proud to hear he was doing well in school. His parents told him that they would be home soon, which made Tobin smile as he choked back tears. Chrissy had to interrupt them and be persistent with Tobin to get him into one of the far corridors. When they stopped Tobin looked back to see his parents fade away.

Tobin turned to look at Chrissy and said with tearful eyes "It's not fair."

Chrissy answered "I know. Let's get you something to eat." Chrissy made sure Tobin had a good meal and followed him back to his quarters. She gave him a kiss on his for head and said "The time storm can't last forever. Don't be sad."

Tobin replied "Don't worry, I have to study. I'll see you tomorrow."

Chrissy looked back as she approached the door "Okay then, don't forget to rest."

Tobin replied as he gathered his books "No, it is time to be lost in thought."

Tobin left Chrissy in the hall and closed his door. Jessy was waiting for Tobin on his bed. Tobin sat down by him and gave him a pat on the head.

Tobin looked at him and said "I was able to see my parents today. I only wish you were there too, so they could have met you. We're going to have to work hard, so you will be able to meet them. I hope soon." Tobin read the information in the books and computer pad, until he fell asleep.

He was wake up by Dent yelling "Tobin." in his quarter's main room.

Tobin got out of bed and came out of his bed room. Tobin asked "What the matter is something wrong."

Dent answered "No. I need you early today. We are doing a new grand opening today, so I need you ready right now."

Tobin blinked his eyes and said "OK."

He grabbed Jessy, gathered his things into his bag, and followed Dent to the shop. The opening went extremely good, the shop was busy all day. When Tobin had a chance, he read one of the books. Later when he was helping customers he would be thinking about the theories he had read. He came to a conclusion that would make his Inner Matter Machine finally work. Tobin worked extra hard getting items asked for by customers, and became exhausted. He seen and met a lot of different people or beings. Tobin even got to wait on David, who was picking up some small crystals. David managed to get Tobin aside to a spot they were not seen. He then gave Tobin a mini holo computer with a list of parts and how to use or assemble them. David told Tobin there are easy guides to the devices they would be building. And that he put a few lessons about time travel on the computer as well for Tobin. The two of them were interrupted by a customer. David wished Tobin well and said that they would meet back on the Gallant at another time. Tobin was left with the customer who didn't even have any idea of what they wanted. The end of the day came quick and they closed the shop.

Dent was excited and told everyone "We did a good job today. And I had a lot of fun. I just don't know about the haggling part, I have a feeling it might grow old. OK then, off with the lot of you. Go get some rest."

Tobin was relieved to hear what Dent said. Tobin wasted no time getting back to his quarters, where he put Jessy down to play. Even though Tobin was hungry, he didn't care. He went to his room and collapsed on his bed. Tobin was so tired he slept straight through to morning.

Jessy woke Tobin up which reminded him that he had to go to the shop, Tobin said aloud "Not yet let's go and get a big breakfast first."

Tobin loaded up his bag and looked at Jessy. "The bag is getting to full; it's time to get the Inner Matter Machine working." Tobin thought to himself. He grabbed the bag and picked up Jessy and carried him in his arms to go and order food. The two of them ate until they couldn't eat another bite.

Tobin sat back in the chair and said to Jessy with

a look of contentment "Now we can go to the shop!"

When Tobin got to the shop Dent and Chrissy were already there, no surprise to Tobin. Dent said to Tobin "'Good morning you look well rested today."

Tobin replied "Sleep does that for a person. I'm ready to sell something that is out of this galaxy!" Tobin looked at Dent with dismay he was wearing a terrible looking suit. Tobin could only guess were Dent had found it.

Dent performed a twirl followed by a bow "What do you think about my outfit?"

Tobin biting his lip said "Look's good on you."

Dent was pleased "I thought as much. Let us connect those travelers with what they may need."

And with that statement their work day began. The day was slow and not too many people came into the shop. Tobin did wait on two odd fellows who used the corner of the shop for their time ship to park. It was made of see through paneling with a glass substance between alternating metal braces and had "phone" printed on the top of it. The two young men referred to everyone as dude. They bought a musical instrument called a guitar and left in a hurry yelling about wild stallions of all things.

When there wasn't much going on Tobin asked Chrissy if she could help him gather the list David gave him. Of course this was only if they were not needed by Dent, Chrissy agreed and said she would start later that night. Tobin thanked her for the help. Later Tobin found a quiet spot in the shop and started working on his Inner Matter Machine. He thought to himself "I'll call it an IM

Box for short."

As he worked on the IM Box a young woman came up to Tobin and asked "What are you working on?" She was skinny, about five and a half feet tall, and had blond hair with red tips. She was wearing blue pants and a short yellow shirt.

Tobin replied "I'm trying to work out the bugs in my Inner Matter Machine."

The girl then said "My name is Misty Solaris, and yours is?"

Tobin looked back up at her "Tobin Guide."

Misty smiled "Pleased to meet you. What does your Inner Matter Box do exactly?"

Tobin continues fiddling with it and replied "It is supposed to take large or small items and reconfigure their matter and store them. The problem with it is I can put items in but when they come out they are missing pieces of them."

Misty looked at the device in Tobin's hands and said "I use something like that when I have to travel."

Tobin stopped and looked up once more "Really?"

Misty outstretched her hand "Yes, let me see yours."

Tobin handed the IM Box and tool to Misty. She fiddled with it for a moment opened it, closed, and finally hit a sequence on an inner panel and closed it. Misty handed the box back to Tobin with a smile and said "That should do the trick." Tobin wasn't sure what to do. Was this a joke? Is she just toying with him? Before he could muster a reply Misty picked up Tobin's figure and put it into the box.

Tobin was nervous and said "Hey."

Misty shushed him and said "It's OK. I reworked its programming and if you're good at programming you could setup a living environment in there."

Tobin was stunned "Are you sure?"

Misty could see his apprehension "Yes." Misty opened the box and pulled out the figure, it was intact with no damaged. She handed the box and figure back to Tobin. And said" So you work here for Anthony Dent?"

Tobin answered as he stared at the IM box "Yes. I help maintain the shop when I have leave from school."

Misty smiled at Tobin "You are a real go getter for a little boy. When, you get older and if you want to time travel, you are always welcome to travel with me."

Tobin stammered "Thank you I would like that, for now I have other things I need to do. Thank you again for your help." Tobin got up and was starting to walk away.

Misty stopped Tobin by tapping him on the shoulder "Oh, well now you can help me. I'm looking for a fossil that is in a shape of a shell. Have you seen it?"

Tobin blushed after almost leaving in a rush "Yes, right this way."

Tobin took her to one of the cabinets. He unlocked it and took out the fossil and re locked the cabinet. Tobin had Misty follow him up to Dent at the register. Dent looked, smiled, and said "What do we have here? Would you like to buy this rock?"

Misty handed him her card and said "Yes, Please."

Dent attempted to be charming "I haven't seen anyone from your region in a long time. How is everyone making it out there? OK I hope."

Misty responded snarky to him by saying "We do just fine, my item please!"

Dent swiped her card and handed it back to her with the fossil. He then said "Have a nice day." Misty said nothing, she just stormed off. Dent looked at Tobin and said "Girls. You never can understand them." Dent adjusted his collar and cuffs on his shirt.

Tobin responded "I thought she was nice."

Dent stared at Tobin shaking his head "You would."

Tobin didn't want to know what Dent meant. He decided to go back to straitening the racks to keep busy.

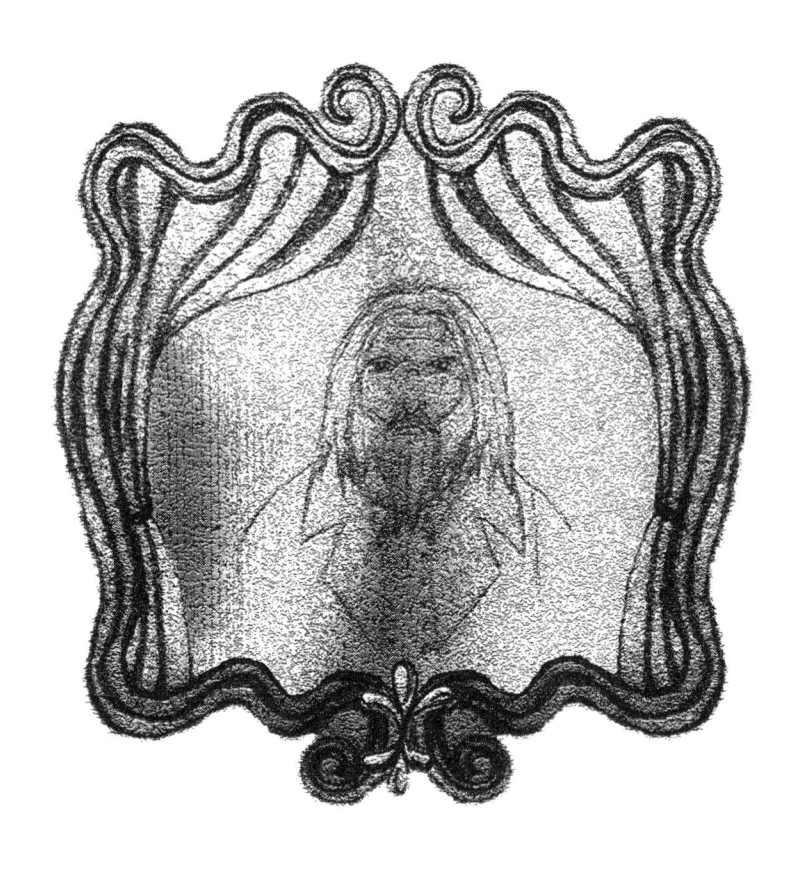

David

Chapter 11

Planet Phoenix

Towards the end of the day Tobin took out the figure and looked at it. He thought to himself you need a name. "I'll call you Midas." he spoke out loud. Tobin got the name from a ship that was in the book he was reading. As Tobin look at Midas he overheard Dent bellowing out "We are closed for the day." Before Tobin could gather his stuff and go for the night Dent came up to him and said "I'd like to have dinner with you. Will you join me?"

Tobin was a bit perplexed but replied "Sure."

Dent seemed pleased "Alright let's go." Dent took Tobin to his personal quarters. When they entered the main room it looked more like a study then living quarters. Dent had maps of star systems and planets on his walls. Some old books were on his shelves and a very old telescope. Dent started with saying "Have a seat over at the table. I already arranged for food to be brought to us."

Tobin nodded and sat himself at the table. Dent walked up to Tobin and tried to start a conversation with him. "You are a quiet one." Tobin watched Dent as he walked away from him and began to fiddle with things around the room. Dent did this until the food was delivered to them. He brought it to the table and laid out the food so they could eat. Tobin thought having the meal with Dent was odd. Dent tried to break the ice again by saying "Do you like working here!"

Tobin replied "Yes, it's not boring like the Gallant."

Dent smiled awkwardly "I like having you here. You are a big help."

Tobin looked towards Dent "I try my best. I'm still disappointed you're not a pirate."

Dent's eyes sparkled as his face lit up "Now that's being a child, like you should be! Not, that grown up you try to be. Wait you thought I was a pirate?"

Tobin chuckled "You did leave that in your notes right?"

Dent's smile turned back to confusion "No. I wrote you were the go to on getting items sold. The customers seem to like you and you know the entire inventory."

Tobin continued to eat as he paused to reply "I came to work for you because Nostalgia is exciting, and has secrets to uncover."

Dent paused with his food hovering between his plate and mouth "It really isn't all that great. I thought traveling time would be more exciting. I'm sure I will have more fun finding these items to sell. But alas I have them now so I better find them owners."

Tobin interjected "Traveling time does seem to be a fun idea but I have to understand it first."

Dent took a napkin to his mouth "All in good time."

After that, they finished there dinner quietly. When they were done eating Dent said to Tobin "You have been working hard and I am worried about you. You seem to be stressed about something. You can tell me if you need."

Tobin remarked "I'm OK. There is nothing to worry about."

Dent seemed nonetheless worried "If it's all the same, I'll be having you go back to your uncle for a while. So you can try and work things out for yourself."

Tobin once again took a somber tone "I don't mind. I have a school project I need to finish."

Dent's brow furrowed "Back to being serious again. Losing your parents made you grow up."

Tobin fighting tears back "No, it only opened my eyes. In my loss I have gained more than I have ever thought. I've stayed in one place long enough to make friends that I truly care about. Nostalgia means a lot to me."

Dent felt pride swell in his chest "I'm honored to be your friend. And you're welcome on Nostalgia any time."

Tobin composed himself "Thanks, if it is all well with you I'd like to go and get some rest."

Dent began to gather the plates "Yes. You should. I'll be sending you back tomorrow after we close the shop."

Tobin gathered together his dishes "OK."

Dent stood as did Tobin "Off with you now."

Tobin smiled a Dent and excused him, while Tobin was going back to his own quarters, he was stopped by Chrissy. Chrissy in a low voice said to Tobin "I heard you're going back tomorrow. I was able to get some items off your list. You want me to get them for you?"

Tobin whispered back "Yes, Bring them to my quarters."

Chrissy was stunned "How are you going to bring them back with you?"

Tobin smiled "Not to worry. I have that figured out already."

Chrissy nodded "OK. I'll see you in a little bit."

The two of them met again in Tobin's quarters. Chrissy helped Tobin pack everything into his I.M. Box before she left him for the night. She commented on how clever he was and wished him well on his project. Tobin thanked her, grabbed up Jessy, and was off to bed.

Tobin had the strangest dreams again and didn't mind waking up early so as to get away from them. He didn't waste time getting ready and with his box working there was room once again for Jessy in the bag. Tobin went to the cafeteria and ordered food to be taken with him. Tobin wanted to eat in the shop, he felt like spending the day there. He thought it might be a while until he'd see the shop. When Dent showed up he was quite surprised to see Tobin early.

Dent commented to him "Are you running a fever

today? You usually show up later."

Tobin shrugged "I just wanted to spend a little bit more time at the shop. After all I need to take mental notes be for I go. I know you'll have it all moved and changed on me by the time I get back."

Dent pondering the thought "Your right. I have grand ideas on what to do with the shop."

Tobin chuckled "You would. Is Chrissy here today?"

Dent scratched his head "I don't think so. It's just us guys today. You should get back to what you were working on the other day."

Tobin grabbed his list "Right."

Tobin went back to where he had his bag set, and noticed Jessy had wondered off. Tobin walked the shop until he found Jessy playing in a box he had found. Tobin started speaking to Jessy "Just how we met the first time. You must love playing in boxes." Tobin took the box and started dragging Jessy in it. This new game Jessy liked and chattered in glee. After that Tobin took pieces of paper crumpled them into balls and threw them for Jessy to chase. Jessy caught onto playing with it quite well. Dent caught Tobin laughing at Jessy when Jessy did a barrel roll chasing the paper.

Dent looked towards where Tobin was and hollered at him "I thought you were to be working."

Tobin answered by yelling back "I said I wanted to spend time in the shop. I didn't say I was going to work."

Dent grumbled under his breath "Even in play he

has to be smart about it."

The day's first customer was an old man looking as if he was dressed like a penguin. A white shirt and black dress coat giving him the look. He was looking for an old pocket watch; Dent had it behind the counter. Dent told Tobin the man was a gentleman's gentleman. What was that supposed to mean to Tobin. Nothing he guessed. Later in this day Marduc came to the shop. Tobin hoped he was there for a visit, but it was business. Marduc needed to pick up a time tumbler and energy cells for a project he was working on. Funny thing Dent had them right in hand for him without any extra wait. Marduc wished Tobin and Dent well and was on his way. Tobin thought to himself, what was Marduc up to. And he pondered is Dent blind not to see something is going on. At the end of the day the two of them closed the shop and went to the shuttle bay.

Before Dent sent Tobin off he said "This parting is only until I send for you again."

Tobin replied "Don't wait to long." Dent gave him a strange look and watched to make sure Tobin boarded the shuttle. "Such an odd boy; was he being serious or was he being smart?" Dent pondered as he watched the shuttle depart.

A week had gone by and Tobin had not seen David anywhere. Being back Tobin had to report to the stations chief and dodge questions from his uncle. Tobin turned in his assignments so as to have the time to do his gathering of the parts. He spent time in his project room assembling the parts per David's instructions. When Tobin finished his assembling the components together he tested the parts to insure they would work. Tobin felt accomplished and took a day off to spend with his uncle. Upon coming back to his project room all the components and parts were missing. Tobin thought it must have been the chief who had taken the parts. That was until he found an electrical note left by day David. It read "Come to the shuttle bay." Tobin made his way unseen to the shuttle bay. David was waiting there for him.

David started with saying "I see you got my note, sorry to alarm you like that. I can't have anyone knowing what we are doing."

Tobin replied "It's OK. I wasn't sure if you were coming back. Is everything the way you needed it?"

David stroked his beard "Yes, you did a perfect job putting them together. We must be going."

Tobin nodded "Yes, understood."

The two of them took a small shuttle to get to a very large ship that was in orbit over the Alpha Phoenix planet. When they arrived David took Tobin up to the bridge of the ship. There David explained what they were going to do, the theory and processes of the project. David said "Pay close attention this is how it is. We are going to set up dark matter containment units on different points on the planet and in different times on the planets time line. We are going to flex link them to the ships core. Then we are going to activate the time capacitor and send a surge of energy to the units through space and time. This will then cause time flux fields to renew the planet and in turn making a newborn Planet."

Tobin remarked "Wow. That's incredible."

David outstretched his hand to Tobin "So, are you with me on this?"

Tobin grabbed his hand in firm manner "Yes."

David and Tobin shook hands "Let's do this."

There was a lot of work to be done. They started by loading containment units into the shuttle. Both David and Tobin had to wear protective suits. It was no easy task trying to find one that would fit Tobin. He had been growing but he was still a ten year old boy. Some of the equipment was heavy and they had to use hydraulic lifters to move them around and put them in place. Tobin liked working with David and wanted to see him get his home back. It was a big job for Tobin but he wasn't alone anymore. They set up the containers and equipment one time line at a time.

The project took the booth of them three months to do; just being the two of them doing a whole crew worth of work. During Tobin's and David's down times they shared stories of loved ones and things they had seen. David had the best stories; he had been more places and seen more thing than Tobin thought he himself would ever see. David took the time to teach Tobin about time travel. David told Tobin what was working time mechanics and not to mistake theories about time as functioning fact. This was because in these theories is where time travelers makes mistakes and can in fact land them stranded in between time and space or on an unknown planet. Tobin got to tour the ship's inner workings on every level.

Tobin was finally able to see what he had been reading about in his studies. A chance to see it work and visually grasp the concept, Tobin took in as much knowledge as he could. He knew this would be the only chance he had to learn firsthand about time travel. Tobin also learned that David had two children and a wife. Tobin was told that they live on a planet that is overpopulated. David's people tend to shy away from living with other races. David was different from the rest of his kind, and wanted to make them their own new but old home. Tobin felt a kinship with David, which made him want to help him even more. At the end when they finished the setup, the two of them stood on the Bridge looking at the planet. It was beautiful sight to see, and it was about to get even more wonderful.

David looked at Tobin and said "Are you ready to do this?"

Tobin replied "It's what we worked for."

David smiled "Then let's make history."

David started the initiation process on the bridge's computer panel. The ships time capacitor started sending them through time, as the core shot out energy to the canister spots. It was an amazing sight with different colors and lights. When the process was over David scanned the planet with the ships computer. He waited and scanned it again. He had a look of dismay on his face.

He turned to Tobin and said "Something's wrong. I don't understand it; nothing has changed. I'll have to go down to the planet and check for myself. Stay here for now Tobin."

Tobin agreed and waited for David's return. When David returned from the planet he had this to say "I don't understand the canisters never activated. The only reason for this is that we didn't have enough power going to them. There is no way this ship can produce that much energy. Not enough to get the job done."

Tobin distressed asked "Is there anything we can do?"

David shook his head as he looked over the calculations "No. Not at the moment. I'll have to reconfigure everything and find a better energy source."

Tobin stared at his distraught friend "What would you have me do?"

David looked to Tobin "At the moment, nothing. You did a great Job. I'll take you back to the Gallant to a point where no one would have missed you."

Tobin put his hand on David's shoulder "I'm sorry it didn't work."

David patted his hand "It's OK. We can try again another time."

David brought Tobin back to the Gallant as he promised. They said their good byes, neither one really wanting to. That night Tobin laid in bed wondering what went wrong and if David could ever save his planet. Tobin also thought is it going to be this kind of disappointment when he tries to get his parents back? With all the different variables with time and space what method was he to us to get his parents back?

"Tobin!!! Tobin!!!" a voice yelled.

Tobin opened his eyes and pushed himself out of bed. He came stumbling out to the main living area to see his uncle holding out Jessy, for Tobin to see. Jessy was covered with baking ingredients along with Stan.

Stan complained to Tobin "Clean your pet up and this mess he made."

Tobin shrugged his shoulders and took Jessy to the bathing room. When Jessy was nice clean and dry, Tobin came out to work on cleaning the rest of the mess.

Tobin figured Jessy must have been hungry they had stayed up late working on another device. Tobin had been getting up late and Jessy didn't like to wait long that for his breakfast. After cleaning up the cooking area Tobin apologized for the mess to his uncle.

Stan answered him by saying "Now you may make our breakfast. Since everything is clean."

Stan then poured himself a cup of coffee and sat to drink it. Tobin sighed and started preparing the food. As he did, he thought responsibility was no fun. They finally sat down to eat after the commotion of the morning.

Stan picked up conversation by saying "Is it your birthday tomorrow?"

Tobin disinterested replied "Yes."

Stan looked up from his meal at Tobin "You look more like thirteen then you do eleven years of age."

Tobin mustered a grin "Must be all those meals you cook."

Stan laughed and said "Or, something in the water could be you're always hiding. I never see you."

Tobin raised an eyebrow "You need to leave the lab to do that."

Stan stammered "I do not spend all my time there."

Tobin looked back down to his meal "We both are busy all day."

Stan clapped his hands together "No excuse, for

us we are going to have a party tomorrow."

Tobin looked up at his uncle "No."

Stan was baffled "No friends to come over?"

Tobin stared blankly at his uncle "That's right. I could stay home for the day if you like."

Stan looked at Tobin "Bonding time?"

Tobin smiled "Maybe."

Stan was thrilled "It's a date."

Tobin old

Chapter 12

All Grown Up

After they ate Stan headed off to the lab and Tobin went to his project room. Tobin looked around the room; everything was where he had left it. Tobin went over to his work bench to check the time device he was working on. He had been building it with spare parts he found, some extra ones Chrissy had given him on Nostalgia and those he hadn't used on David's devices. Tobin fiddled with it for a moment and made a few adjustments. The concept of the device is to slow down time. It was a prototype and was only to work on a small area for five minutes for a test. Tobin thought if it indeed did work he could build a bigger one and use it to slow down the time storm so his parents ship the Rochelle could fly out of its grasp to the current time.

"So this is it." Tobin thought to himself. "It's time to test it. Will it work?" Tobin was nervous he, made sure Jessy and Midas were out of range. He took the device to a far corner, and then set the timer on it to go off in three minutes. Tobin went and stood back by Jessy to watch the timer go off. Tobin thought he would just throw a ball through the field to see if it would suspend or slow down the movement of the ball.

Tobin waited three minutes and then throws the

ball; nothing happened to the ball. It bounced against the wall and rolled back to him. Then Tobin walked up to the device to see why it didn't activate. He told Jessy to stay put. He then picked up the device to check the timer, as Tobin was looking the device over suddenly it activated. It sent out a surge of energy pushing Tobin backwards knocking him unconscious. Tobin woke up to Fauna gentling nudging him.

Tobin was a bit disorientated and asked "What happened?"

Fauna replied "That is what I was going to ask you." Fauna helped Tobin sit up and looked him over.

Tobin asked "Is Jessy OK?"

Fauna answered "Your pet. Yes. He is OK."

Tobin sighed in relief "Good."

Fauna took a stern tone "Exactly what were you doing?"

Tobin still trying to gain his bearings "Working on a time device I think it broke."

Fauna helped Tobin to steady himself "It did more than that. Your device sent an energy surge that crashed our systems on the station for a minute. When they came back online I had the systems administrator trace where the surge came from. That's how I knew to come to you."

Tobin rubbed his aching head "Oh that makes sense."

Fauna smiled "Come on let's get you to the infirmary."

Tobin still disoriented "Yeah I did hit my head a good one."

With the help of Fauna Tobin stood up; he notice Fauna seemed smaller to him. Tobin felt dizzy and started to pull at his shirt it was tight fitting. Fauna brought Tobin to her personal physician, who started treating him immediately.

Tobin asked in fear "How bad did I hit my head?"

Fauna answered "It's not that. You know how tomorrow happens to be your eleventh birthday?"

Tobin looked at Fauna attempting to focus "Yes."

Fauna tried to keep calm "It's going to be more like your eighteenth birthday."

Tobin snapped out of his haze "I really messed things up."

Fauna placed her hand on his forehead "Don't worry just lay back and take it easy. I sent for your pet and uncle. I just have to figure a way to tell your uncle what had happened."

Tobin laid back and mumbled "OK."

When Stan arrived at the infirmary he had a worried look on his face. Fauna walked up to him, but before she could say anything, Stan walked right past her.

Stan walked up to Tobin and said "You look just like your father at that age. And you just went from the "I want to know everything" age to the "I know everything and I'm not listening to you age.""

Fauna interrupted by saying "That's uncalled for. If you would let me explain what happened."

Stan turned to Fauna "You don't need too. I'm one of your top researchers. I can see what has happened. Tobin has been in my care for the last four years. You don't think I know he is different and why? You don't need to hide things from Tobin or me."

Fauna put her hands behind her back "I guess we need to work this matter out."

Tobin didn't know what to think about what was going on, Fauna insisted on Tobin resting. After Tobin had napped and the doctor took his vitals he was allowed to go with Stan to Fauna's office.

When in the office Fauna started off with, "This is how it is, Tobin was doing independent studies on time travel and he thought he could go back and be with his parents."

Stan remarked "Fauna you're really bad at making things up. I know about the time storm and who caused it." Stan paused and looked at Tobin. And went on to say "Your parents were lost in the time storm but it wasn't the first time they encountered it. When your mother was pregnant for you their ship entered and left the time storm. And that's how I know the storm would draw you back to it someday."

Tobin's mind was swimming in confusion; it was one of those times he didn't know what to do. He spoke up "I'm not ready to be an adult."

Fauna interjected "No one is, but you took on the responsibility of an adult."

Stan interrupted by saying "Give him some room

to think. Tobin getting your parents back isn't your responsibility. In case you do try and get them back. Don't just do it for yourself do it for me as well."

Tobin responded shaking his head in shame "I've done everything wrong so far."

Stan corrected Tobin "You went about it wrong. Yes, that part is true. It isn't that time needs to be slowed down. You need to stop the event that caused the time storm."

Tobin was lost "So, what do I do?"

Stan looked to Tobin and then to Fauna "I don't know and I would never try to do it myself. But we can take you to the person who started all this. He would be the only one who could help you. I only wish I had better prepared you for life."

Tobin felt a tinge of sorrow "You did the best job. I should have listened to you more."

Stan smiled at Tobin "We can make it right." Stan wrapped his arms around Tobin and gave him a tight hug. Stan looked at Fauna and said "You will have to take him there."

Fauna motioned for Tobin to follow her and replied "I know it can't be any other way."

Tobin was going up in the elevator lift as he done so often. Tobin could only stand and wait as Fauna escorted him. This wasn't the normal kind of visit to the shop for Tobin. The doors opened, the two of them entered the shop, and walked up to the counter.

Dent was standing over by a rack of clothes talking to a tall, skinny man, with a rather large chin.

Tobin could over hear Dent saying "Speaking loudly, fast, and quickly waving your arms around does not impress me."

The man retorted "It works on everyone else."

Dent held up his hand to the man's face to stop him "It's ignorant, childish, and bow ties are truly overrated." Dent noticed Fauna and Tobin so he left the man with these parting words. "Be gone with you. I have customers to attend to." With that done Dent left the man to ponder his words and came over to Fauna and Tobin. He started by saying "Is there anything I can help you find or do for you?"

Fauna replied "Yes, there is. Tobin here has questions for you?"

Dent looked at the young man before him "How strange? Is that this young man's name?"

Tobin spoke up "It's me Tobin. Tobin Guide." Tobin opened his bag and pulled out Jessy to show Dent his identity.

Dent a little baffled said "Now come on. It wasn't that long ago that I last sent for you. Was it?"

Dent started pacing back and forth racking his brain to find an answer.

Tobin answered Dent, causing him to pause "No. I made a mistake and we came here to see if you could help me."

Dent snapped his fingers "Come then to my office."

Tobin stunned "You have an office?"

Dent looked back at Tobin with an odd smile "Yes, were else do you think I hide."

It was a small cozy room they entered. It had a lounger and couch that looked like Dent had spent more time on it then his own bed. There was also a viewing screen and computer. Dent being a good host said "Have a seat. Can I get you anything to drink?"

Tobin responded "I'm fine."

Fauna added "Same here. So let's talk about the mess you caused Dent."

Dent protested "I had nothing to do with Tobin's condition."

Fauna shouted "Yes, you did. You were the one who caused the time storm that took Tobin's parents."

Dent shot a glare at Fauna "That is something that I wish I could undo. I must have thought of hundreds of ways, but none that would work."

Tobin trying to explain said "I was trying to slow down time. To see if it would work and if I could use it on the time storm. Instead I sped up time and aged myself by seven years."

Dent looked back to Tobin scolding him as he said "You should have not been messing with time. Fauna you let this happen, you should be blaming yourself for it. Tobin if you wanted to know about time travel you should have come to me."

Tobin replied "You are the first friend I ever had. I felt if I asked you, that you would have left me or sent me away like everyone else. I was just trying to fix everything. I want to help Chrissy and get my parents back."

Dent turned his back to Tobin and Fauna clenching his fist as he pressed it against the wall "I hate to see Chrissy the way she is, as much as you do. But there is not a thing we can do. If the time storm is altered it would make it grow bigger, not stop it. And as for your condition Tobin it can't be reversed. To undo the acceleration done to you would damage your cells and cut your life span in half. I can't let you do anything like that."

Tobin saddened yet curious asked "Dent tell me are you really the one who caused the time storm?"

Dent once again turned to look Tobin in the eyes "I wish I could say no. This is how it all happens or began if you will. Marduc and I were studying together under a professor called Gozen. We were on a station called the St. Augustus not far from Professor Gozen's home planet Alpha Centaury. Alpha Centaury was the object of our studies or more over how to save it. There was a plasmatic energy cluster destroying the planet's atmosphere and would eventually destroy the planet. It did despite Marduc and my best efforts. The three of us planned on saving the planet by moving it. We had found a dead planet to replace it with so as not to change gravitational pulls in the star system or planet. This would take great power to do so; we would use the station as a conductor and the cluster as the power source. We thought the theory was sound but as we were putting in the last configurations. I found there to be a space station near the dead planet with over a thousand people on it. If we went through with the plan it would destroy the station in the process. I couldn't let that happen I told the Professor to stop the program he would not listen. I tried to stop him but he had me and

Marduc locked up.

The Professor executed the plan, at first it seemed to work. In the middle of the presses everything stopped, the planet had not moved or the cluster. When the Professor let Marduc and I go, I left to see what had happened to the station by the dead planet. When I had arrived I discovered the people had left the station. Do to it being in disrepair and the cluster had left a time storm around the station that would come and go. It traps ships."

Tobin stopped Dents speech by saying "The planet you were going to replace was the Phoenix planet. And that means I have to succeed were you had failed."

Dent threw up his hands "Haven't you been listening, if you try to alter the storm it will get worse. I am not going to let you hurt yourself again."

Tobin crossed his arms "I'm listening. I'm going to follow my uncle's advice."

Dent smiled at what he heard "Good about time you listen to common sense. Tobin I would like for you to stay here with me. In case your condition worsens I can get you treatments that you would need. Is that going to be OK?"

Tobin glanced back to Fauna "Its OK."

Fauna nodded "Yes that should be fine."

Tobin said "Can I go? I need to think and a good walk is what I need right now."

Dent answered "Yes. That will be fine."

After Tobin had left the room Fauna asked Dent

"Have you seen Trill?"

Dent shook his head no and said "She is not welcome on this station."

Fauna looked at Dent sternly "Not by the space and time signatures I've read."

Dent rubbed his temple "It must be Trace's doing."

Trill

Chapter 13

Trill

Tobin had Jessy walking with him they wandered the halls and corridors of Nostalgia. Tobin was not sure what to do? Everything had happened so fast. He felt scared, unsure, and alone. He could not believe the mess he got himself into. Tobin thought about what to do. Dent and Fauna were not going to help him. What about Chrissy could she help? Tobin heard voices, causing him to forget his thoughts and follow them.

He came to an unused docking bay were, he seen Trace talking to a brunette woman. The woman was wearing a white shirt, black flight jacket, and black leather pants. The two of them went in to one of the other side rooms to finish talking as Tobin snuck into the bay. Tobin seen a diamond shaped ship and without hesitation took the opportunity to use the ship. He grabbed up Jessy and his bag and climbed into the ship. It was rather small, but it would do.

As the door close Tobin belted in and said "Time to go to where this all started." To Tobin's surprise no sooner did the ship start it stopped and the door opened. Tobin grabbed his bag and climbed out of the ship thinking it must be under repairs. But Tobin wasn't in the stations bay anymore. He found himself in what appeared to be a holding area with only one door. As Tobin walked up to it, he noticed the ship was gone.

Tobin said as he opened the door "This looks like the only option." He opened the door and stepped into a luxurious lounge room. It had potted trees, lounge chairs, benches, and a miniature water fall.

Tobin was in awe of the beauty and to himself said "This place looks great. I wonder who stays here." Tobin heard the door open and panicked, where to hide was the solitary thought ran through his head.

Tobin heard a woman's voice say "Hello there."

Tobin turned around to see the woman who had been talking to Trace. She went on to say "Don't Panic. You're in no danger." Tobin was trembling not really knowing why.

The lady went on "Have you seen a ghost or are you going to cry? My name is Trill and yours is?"

Tobin swallowed hard and said "Tobin."

Trill said with reassuring smile "I have heard a lot about you. And what brings you here?"

Tobin frantically stammered "I don't know? I made a mistake."

Trill tried to calm Tobin "There is never a mistake. You meant what you did."

Tobin blurted "I'm sorry for taking your time ship."

Trill chuckled "Time ship no. It is a transit time pod and this is the central hub. Oh apology accepted."

Tobin confused "Where is this place?"

Trill outstretched her arms "We are in a fold in time. The people who made this place were very advanced."

Tobin stumbled to find words "Where are they now?"

Trill lowered her arms to her side "They found a religion to follow that didn't believe in using time travel. So they abandoned this whole station."

Tobin's curiosity gets the better of him "How did you find it?"

Trill giggled "I made a mistake, got lost, and found this wonderful place. Now I have a question for you. Are you supposed to be a ten year old? You look older than that to me."

Tobin sheepishly replied "I miscalculated on a time experiment, Dent said there still may be after effects and my condition could worsen."

Trill laughed "He is full of it. Not true at worse some headaches. I knew a time traveler who had an assistant that had the same thing happen. She was just fine. But I can tell you not a good way to get a girlfriend your own age now!"

Tobin stifled a laugh "You know a lot. Are you the supplier Dent doesn't like and stopped using?"

Trill rolled her eyes "Yes, but I still fill his orders through Trace. The old Dent and I are good friends and he ordered me to keep bringing supplies to Nostalgia no matter what."

Tobin confused "Dent doesn't trust you, why? You seem nice?"

Trill grinned at Tobin "Dent has good reason not to. I stole his time machine and left Dent stranded on a planet."

Tobin alarmed "I see. May be I should be going."

Trill could sense his distrust "No don't worry. The old Dent and I patched things up. The young Dent doesn't know it yet."

Tobin quickly changed the subject "OK what do you do?"

Trill struck a dramatic pose "I'm a time bandit."

Tobin raised an eyebrow in disbelief "Not a pirate?"

Trill thought about it "No but that does sound fun."

Tobin smiled he was starting to relax. Trill then offered "Would you like some hot cocoa, come up to the control room with me?"

Tobin replied "Yes."

Walking through the station was much nicer than any Tobin had seen in his life. None of the lessons he had studied ever showed anything of this magnitude of beauty. When they arrived at the control room Trill served the drinks and they sat down. She even gave a treat to Jessy. Tobin was looking around the room taking in every detail when something nipped his leg. He looked down to see a large reptile crawl out of underneath the control panel. It had an emerald green shell, a flat dark head, and eight legs with tufts of hair upon them.

Tobin yelled out "What is that."

Trill answered "It's my pet spider turtle. His name is Gamma. I'm sure he didn't mean to scare you."

Tobin alarmed "OK hmm, is it nice?"

Trill smiled as she fed a treat to Gamma "Yes all he does is lay around all the time. He just wanted to check you out."

Tobin chuckled a little "Is that the only pet you have?"

Trill looked at Tobin "Yes. Also why did you run away from Nostalgia?"

Tobin paused then said "I want to stop the time storm."

Trill winked at Tobin "I thought so. I'll help you."

Tobin was surprised "Why?"

Trill's face dimmed "I too have lost a parent. My mother is Fauna and she can't stop or alter anything because of her job. When my father was murdered she could do nothing about it. And that's when I did it; I took Dent's ship and went after the man who killed my father. I didn't have the heart to kill the Professor named Gozen. But I made him disappear to where he couldn't hurt anyone anymore."

Tobin was alarmed "Was he the same Professor Gozen?"

Trill nodded "Yes all the more reason to help you.

How about you tell me your side of everything and what you have done so far."

Tobin obliged her and told Trill how he met Dent, stole a shuttle, talked to Fauna and his uncle. About his time device and that he helped David.

Trill then told Tobin "If what you are saying is true. You are half way there, to get rid of the storm."

Tobin was stunned "I really am?"

Trill stretched and yawned "Yes after we get some relax time in and recharge our batteries. I will tell you what we are going to do."

Tobin looked dumbfounded at Trill "OK but I don't have a battery."

Trill giggled "You are too funny! It just means get some rest."

Tobin went and found a soft lounger to sleep on. Trill gave him a blanket and watched over him until he dosed off. When Tobin woke up he found a plate of fruit and a glass of juice left for him. Without question Jessy and Tobin ate all the fruit. Tobin was feeling better about everything now. Now that he found Trill he was sure things were looking up. Trill had happened to check on Tobin as he just finished eating.

She smiled and said "You look much better. Are you ready to help me call in some favors?"

Tobin replied "Favors?"

Trill put her hand on her hip and cocked her head "You don't think we can do this by ourselves do you?"

Tobin took a deep breath "What are we going to do?"

Trill explained "The Phoenix planet needs more energy and I know where there is a plasma cluster to fuel it."

Tobin tilted his head "You mean the one at St. Augustus."

Trill tapped her finger to the bridge of her nose "Yes but we need David's ship. And he is hard to get a hold of. That's why we're going to go find him right?"

Tobin smiled and stood up "Right."

Tobin grabbed Jessy and his bag then followed Trill to a big room It had a large machine in it, that had gears all over it.

Tobin asked "What is that for?"

Trill replied "It's a time machine, I just have it disguised. You know that there are different types?"

Tobin flustered replied "I know."

Trill circled the machine pointing to various gears "This one is fun to operate; it has different time rhythms for each section of the ship. If you don't line them up right you will end up arriving at the destination with only half your ship. Not highly recommended."

Tobin shook his head "Oh boy..."

The insides were much nicer than those of the time pod. Tobin could understand the control panels much easier, though they were put in odd places.

Trill started with "Now this ship doesn't need a

bay for docking. It does not lift off it only has to warm up and it can start jumping through the time lines any questions?"

Tobin replied "How long have you known Dent and how did you meet?"

Trill was amused "You're courageous. Dent was registering to be a time traveler. My mother pointed him out to me and said stay away from that man, he is nothing but trouble. That is all it took for me to run off and travel with him. Adventure and the unknown beckoned me. That was until, I heard about my father."

Tobin wanted to know more "Is Trill your real name."

Trill looked back at Tobin "Nickname, my real name is Paz Trillium."

Tobin blushed "It's a pretty name. How do you register to be a time traveler?"

Trill was amused "You are full of questions. Most travelers are born into the trade. You can go through training for it if say Fauna vouches for you. OK, mister chatty we're there."

Tobin looked at Trill "Already?"

Trill got up from her seat "Yep, out you go."

When Trill and Tobin came out of the ship they entered a huge city, a vast array of buildings spread out before them. The horizon was a deep crimson red sky and there was smoke coming from the foundries on the planet. The air smelled terrible; almost nauseating. The buildings were tall, close together, and seemed to keep the smoke trapped about their peaks.

Tobin coughed and said "What is this place?"

Trill answered with a rasp "Prefect Nine, it is an industrial planet. They make the finest ships here and like most planets it's overpopulated."

Tobin gagged "It smells terrible!"

Trill eyes were starting to water "Yes it does, alright keep close to me. We'll go to the scrap yard first. We need to ask if they've seen David."

Tobin rubbed his stinging eyes "Will do."

They walked part of the city, it was dirty and crowded. The smoke seemed to coat everything it reached. Despite this Tobin was still in awe of everything he seen. There were shops everywhere, but none like the ones on Nostalgia. He noticed places, to many different places to eat and more for entertainment. That was a thought for Tobin, to entertain one's self instead of studying.

As they walked Trill asked "This is your first time on a populated planet?"

Tobin commented back "Yes, it is an interesting place, but it's not a place for me."

Trill smiled "You prefer stations?"

Tobin shrugged "I don't know yet."

The two of them came up to a large gate with a window. A guard was on the other side watching them as they came up. Trill went up to the man and talked for a minute and then came back to Tobin.

She then said "We're in luck; David is in the yard

right now. That saves us a lot of trouble. The guard will let us in to see him"

They entered the gate to see piles of parts all over the yard. Trill guided Tobin through the mess until they found David. David was picking over some more new looking parts. He spotted Trill and Tobin right away and stopped what he was doing.

David came up to them and said "Trill it's good to see you and who is your friend."

Trill replied with a wide grin "You should know him, this is Tobin."

David looked towards Tobin and said "My boy you grew up."

Trill looked at Tobin "Yes he did; into a sharp looking young man."

David teasingly scolded Trill "Oh, I think you made him blush. What brings the two of you here?"

Trill whispered in David's ear "I would like to call in a favor."

David looked Trill in the eyes and asked "What does this favor require?"

Trill thought for a moment "Oh, not much you, your ship, thermal time disrupters, a plasmatic cluster, regenerating a planet, stopping a time storm, and saving over a billion life forms."

David chuckled "Is a tall favor you ask and I'm seeing where you are going with this. It's a good thing you came to me for the help; anyone else would mess it up."

Trill winked at David "Absolutely right! You are the smartest man I known."

David straightened his beard "I'll meet you on my ship, it is in orbit. I have to gather these parts before I go."

Trill pointed at David "It's a date see you there. Come along Tobin we have missions."

Tobin smiled at David and nodded to Trill.

Gamma

Chapter 14

Team Work

Tobin and Trill left David and made their way back to the ship. As they were getting ready to leave Tobin asked "Are we going to do all that?"

Trill smiled at Tobin "Yes we are, it is in the fates; our destiny."

Tobin asked in a stern manner "Dent told you to do all this didn't he?"

Trill's face took a more somber tone "Maybe."

Tobin looked at Trill with distrust in his eyes "You know the outcome?"

Trill looked to Tobin "I know more than one possible outcome with similar results."

Tobin's tone eased up "We have to be careful or we'll cause a time line split."

Trill nodded "That's right; I'm only going by a guideline. It's up to us to make the right choices."

They sat quietly as Trill started the ship and prepared to dock with David's ship. Tobin curiously asked "Why have we not docked yet?"

Trill replied "Waiting for David. His ship is set up so you have to have permission to dock. He has an advanced system setup that will not allow just any time traveler from any time to have access to his ships docking bay. David has to enter a code so I can finish the ships course.

Tobin inquired "Does Nostalgia have the same system?"

Trill pondered for a moment "It has one similar to it. Dent has his setup more free and open for his customers. He still can block ships of his choice that's why I have all his codes."

Tobin laughed lightly "You're sneaky."

Trill snickered at the thought "We're in, you may exit the ship."

When Trill and Tobin entered the bay, David was waiting for them. David rolled his eyes at Trill and said "You are still using Dent's old junky machine."

Trill replied "I haven't fixed the probability drive in the other one yet. And this old thing still works fine."

David "I shouldn't even let it on board. Pretty sure that thing is dirtier than my work clothes. Oh well, let's get down to the nitty gritty of the afar."

Trill got out a holo pad and began "To start we need your ship to be in orbit over Alpha Phoenix before the time storm was caused. Then we make adjustments to your ship to turn it into a big energy conductor and aim it at the planet's surface. The next step is to place the thermal time disrupters into the path that would become the time storm, and the final steps will be taken on St. Augustus.

David intently stroked his beard as he stated "I see but who would come back to man my ship?"

Trill tapped her finger tips together "Let me tend to that. I have the most important part of the mission on yours and Tobin's shoulders."

David paused in mid stroke of his beard "Hmm?"

Tobin interjected "Will the thermal time disrupters stop the storm from happening?"

Trill answered "No the use of them will cause the time storm to dissipate. We can't stop the time storm because it will change the events in your life Tobin. By setting up the thermal time disrupters you can travel time to the end of the storm and be with your parents again."

Tobin confused "Do you know when that is?"

Trill tilted her head "We will know after our mission, when that will be projected in the outcome."

Tobin face fell blank "All this is going to be is a cross your fingers kind of thing."

Trill paused and asked "Will you still take the chance."

Tobin thought for a moment and answered "Yes."

Tobin and Trill looked into each other's determined eyes as silence fell about them.

David interjected "Come you two there is plenty to be done. We can start with adding receivers to my ship."

With that said the three of them started gathering

the components for the receivers. The three worked together as if they trained for the task together for years. Even though they had different ways of doing things, they somehow complimented each other's skills. The receivers were built and attached to the ship. After that they rewrote the programs on the bridge console to receive and project the energy. The last step was to set the projector and angle of the energy to the planet. Tobin was astonished at the work they did.

As they had finished Trill said "Now we have to head out to St. Augustus. David you can join Tobin and I in my ship."

David with protest in his voice "Travel in a death trap you can't even call it a ship."

Trill smirked at David as she motioned to his communicator "You have another time ship or are you going to call Dent up and ask for a ride?"

David sighed and crossed his arms "OK I'll go with you since you think you know what you're doing."

Trill motioned David toward the ship's helm "You can drop me off back at your ship later. You should get used to the controls on my ship. I'm sure you can manage."

David looked at the controls with a wary eye from the entry port "Right, there's no time like the present."

Trill opened up the storage area "Let's gear up."

David being huffy took his is time getting in the ship and seated. David seemed to act as though the ship was an anomaly of time waiting to collapse upon its self. Tobin couldn't see what the problem was; he liked seeing different ships. The other thing he thought was did David not like Dent? Despite David's discomfort, the three arrived at St. Augustus. They had no mechanical failures contrary to David's opinion on the flight. When they entered the station there was barley any power to it. The auxiliary lights flickered and the silence was bone chilling. Each step the three took echoed for what seemed to be an eternity. The air was thin and it looked abandoned. They made their way to the main control room. To Tobin's surprise Marduc was waiting there for them.

With a warm greeting "Good to see that you made it here I have already started setting up the cells and crystal."

Tobin said in an excited voice "Marduc you were in on this the whole time? And that's why you were sneaking around Nostalgia to get parts for this station?"

Marduc smiled at Tobin "Yes you found me out. The only thing is due to your watch full eye, I had not been able to get all the parts I was after."

Tobin slapped his hand to his forehead "Oops. You lead me to be believed you were up to something devious."

Marduc bowed his head some "I don't come across well to others. Some people close to me would have understood. As a result I'm going to have to ask you and David to go back to Nostalgia to pick up the rest of the parts."

David chimed in with a grumble "Nice but the credits on my card have already been spent."

Trill resolved the problem by saying "Use mine it will have more than enough."

David skeptical "Dent will ask why I have your card."

Trill ever confident said "Say I owe you and you can't wait for a transfer."

David shrugged "We'll see if it flies. Tobin can vouch for me; right Toby?"

Tobin a bit unsure, "Yes. I'm sure I could do that. Is that supposed to be a nickname?"

David let forth a bellowing laugh "You don't like it? OK how about T.G. or something else."

Tobin frowned "No Tobin is a fine name."

David turned to Marduc hand outstretched "Marduc lets have that list."

Marduc gave David a computer pad then said "Good luck to you. When you get back I'll let you know how we are coming along and what you can do."

Trill motioned with her hand "You can take my ship. I'll stay and see how far Marduc got with my instructions."

David with a sigh "Very well then come Tobin let us see if I can stomach flying that ship."

With a pause David was on his way out the door with Tobin on his heels. As Tobin walked with David he asked "Do you not like Dent?"

David answered in a rushed manner "He is a fine man. He just isn't up to my caliber of skills. I will give him one compliment he does know how to get what you need to you. Though I think that has a lot to do with Trill's help. I guess Dent does have good foresight something he picked up through his journeys no doubt."

Tobin looked to David with a smile "I like working for him I've seen so many new things."

David smiled back "You would see even more if you became a time traveler."

Tobin's smile faded "I have no ship; I would just like to have my parents back and safe."

David paused and turned to Tobin placing his hands upon his shoulders "You are very noble Tobin and if you were my son I would be very proud. I have faith we can make this happen."

The two of them made their way back to the ship. With grumbling under his breath David put in the coordinates into the control panel. It only took a few minutes to get to the abandoned part of Nostalgia. There was no one in the bay to greet them. David began to explain to Tobin "Looking at this list I can say we will have to deal with Dent directly. I need you to play coy and go along with what I say. I timed our arrival a half hour after you left in Trills pod. Dent won't be aware of you leaving. I'll tell him I ran into you and you're helping me find the items I'm looking for. Got that all down?"

Tobin shook his head "Yes."

The two made their way to the shop, the place looked rather dim. They found Dent looking at a graph on a holo computer. David wasted no efforts in smooth talking Dent. Dent left and came back with the items they needed. Dent gave two totes to David and ran the card.

Dent then said "David you have helped me in the

past. But I do have to question your means and motives at this point." Dent turned to Tobin and said "I have picked up some strange magnetic readings around the station. Help David take his items to his ship. After that I need you to come back here. I have to lock down the station for safety measures."

Tobin replied "Yes I understand."

Dent watch as the two picked up the totes and left. As they walked back to the ship David said to Tobin. "Sounds like the thermal time disrupters are working; we soon will see the results. No matter what we can't turn back now. We have to finish Trills plan. I hope she knows what she is doing, because we won't have much time. Everything has to be done exact or this will be a mess."

Tobin gulped "If I wasn't worried before I am now."

David said as they arrived back at the bay. "I only hope that storm doesn't mess with our trip back to St. Augustus."

Tobin fearfully replied "Me too."

Tobin and David loaded the totes and settled into the ship. As David was afraid of the ship would go off course only to realign back. It did take longer to get back to the station with luck they did get there. After unloading the totes on to a dolly, David looked at a device that was on his forearm.

Tobin noticed David looking at the device and asked "Is that some sort of a time keeping device?"

David looked up from the device and answered "Yes it is in fact all time travelers have one. What it does is puts off a field around us and who ever we are with. This Field in turn lets us remember anything that has been changed in the time stream. We call them T.I.P.'s for short but they are Time Index Pedometer. They are used for recording path, actions, outcome, and memories of all the time travelers wearing them."

Tobin scratched his head trying to comprehend "You mean what we are doing and about to do?"

David nodded to Tobin "Yes."

Tobin looked distressed "That means Dent will remember and know what we have done."

David let out a sigh "Yes the mission does not go without consequences. Dent may not be our friend when we come back. In fact we are about to become time bandits like Trill and probably have to answer to the Time Watchers Committee."

Tobin attempted to muster a smile "That's great at least Trill has plenty of extra rooms for us to stay in."

David grabbed the dolly and the two of them brought it to the main control room. As Marduc was waiting for them, he was typing a program.

Marduc looked up and said "Ah perfect your here. I just got done writing St. Augustus's new program. I'm sure the two of you will have no problem installing it. Trill is setting up the time receivers."

Tobin asked "Why don't you install the program here?"

Marduc was stunned "I forgot you're not in the loop of things yet. Let me explain it to you we are doing changes to the station here in the future. These changes are to the hardware. We are turning it into a conductor to sling shot the plasmatic cluster to Alpha Phoenix. This will pass by Nostalgia safely no one will be hurt in the process. When we have the adjustments setup and ready to go we are going to use time tumblers and send them back in time to before the event the professor caused. Now the program I have made will overwrite the Professor's program and any commands he gives. And it will install its self, putting in the trajectories we need to sling shot the energy. This is the tricky part I need you Tobin and David to go back in time to install the program. Neither Trill nor I can do this. If we did it would gum up time and space. Dent and I do not meet either one of you two until later in our lives. So, the two of you are the perfect fix."

David responded as he checked his T.I.P. once more "I see your point."

Tobin chimed in with "Is this going to be dangerous?"

David looked back to Tobin and replied "That's why there are stun blasters."

Tobin sighed at the thought "I Just felt a heavy weight put upon me."

Marduc interrupted "The two of you will do fine. There isn't' much as far as security on the station. How about you two go and get those cores up to Trill. She is on the top deck. And I'll upload the program to a computer pad for you."

Tobin and David gathered up the cores and went to the top deck. Where they found Trill in frustration, throwing a screw driver on the floor. The screwdriver rolled past them. The two walked up to her and David asked "What's the matter?"

Trill huffily said "I'm trying to attach these wires and transistors to this module. There isn't enough room to work and my hands are not small enough. Wait, you know if I had the hands of a ten year old bet I could finish this."

Tobin interjected "Smart idea but I have something better."

Tobin opened his bag where he spots Jessy sleeping. All the time traveling was tending to do that to the little guy making him easy to handle. Tobin put his hand alongside Jessy in the bag. "Ah there it is" he thought, in his hand he pulled out his figure Midas. Tobin took it over to where Trill was working and set it down. It came to life and Tobin showed Midas how to hold the wires in place. It was in the perfect spot for Trill. Trill picked up her tools and started working. When she was finished she patted Midas on the head and thanked him.

Trill turned to Tobin and said "Your really are good at this. You know I have connections and I could get you registered as a time traveler. When all is said and done you could start your training, all you have to do is take some tests. Then you need to travel with a certified trainer. And vow to obey the Time Watchers Committee's code."

Tobin grinned at Trill and said "Must be a hard code to follow. I'm in so much trouble as it is, I'll be lucky to see a life remotely close to the one I had. For now I'll pass."

Trill shrugged "You know what's best for yourself. I will not question you. Can the two of you help me set up the rest of the equipment while you're here?"

David brushed his beard straight with his hands and answered "No problem, point the way."

Working on St. Augustus was strange. Tobin kept feeling like he was being watched. He wasn't one for believing ghost stories, but if he was ever to see one it would most likely be here. Tobin noticed they were putting parts on equipment that didn't work. He thought to himself "I hope this stuff works in the past in." Tobin couldn't wait to get off the station; the thin air was making him light headed. After they had finished installing the parts, equipment, and time tumblers the four of them met in the main control room. Trill took a moment alone with David after that it was decided they would rest and have refreshments for a little while.

Marduc started off by saying "I have put everything you need to know on this computer pad. You have the exact coordinates to a safe bay for docking and the time to land. I have a map of the station that shows the port to upload the program too. Your blasters are in the ship already and lastly I've loaded all the access and security codes you will need. I suggest locating the port while here it will also help when you go back so you will know right where it is at. When the program is uploaded it will do all the work. You two only have to stay long enough to make sure the program goes through and starts up. When it is safe make your way back to Nostalgia. I've uploaded the exact time the storm will be gone and when your parents will be arriving at the Gallant. Trill and I both ran the calculations and figures."

Tobin gave thought to everything that was said "So we do pull off the plan? Why are we using a computer pad?"

Trill looked to Tobin "The computer pad is less likely to get damaged in time travel over a holo computer. As for the plan we really don't know, with what we have done so far. The time storm will dissipate and Nostalgia will be safe. But we don't know the outcome of the two planets. Even if I try I can't cheat at knowing everything."

Tobin agreed "OK I get it, we can't control the fates."

David still contemplating asked "What about my ship?"

Trill looked at David sternly "I'll man the ship and program."

David's face fell solemn "Really?"

Trill looked away "I'll have Marduc drop me off."

David rubbed his temples "You know by using my ship as a conductor the energy will obliterate it. There is no time ship that would be fast enough to get you out of the way of the blast."

Tobin cried "What?"

Trill stopped him by saying "I know the risks. You can't gain anything if you're not willing to lose something. Don't worry I have it covered."

Trill rolled up her coat sleeve revealing a modified device with a miniature time tumbler.

David sneered at her and said "That little toy of yours will not get you far."

Trill responded firmly "I just have to get to the Gallant or Nostalgia. It will get me there."

Tobin spoke up with "Is that what you meant by

not knowing all the outcomes. You don't know if you are going to make it back; or any of us for that matter."

Trill looked to Tobin with teary eyes "I owe a debt to the universe so consider this paying it off."

Tobin looked at David and said "You're not going to let her do the mission are you David?"

David got out of his chair and went up to Trill. He took her arm and looked at the device she made. David took a tool out of his pocket and adjusted the device.

David then in assurance said "Hmm its sound. What you got there will do the job. You have to get the timing just right. There will be a second or two delays. So leave yourself room. You didn't get the idea for this device from Dent did you?"

Trill laughed and said "No I ran across a guy called Jack. He had a similar device, didn't catch what he called it. When I made mine I made sure it had a better battery source. Still don't know what to call it. But it will let a person travel space and time to some extent."

Marduc interjected "This is all good and fine. If we are done fretting over what is being done. We need to finish it. David and Tobin you should go and walk this path you'll take before you leave. Off with you two. Go and gather your thoughts."

Tobin looked at Trill with a sad face, Trill came up to him patted his shoulder. Then whispered to him "It's OK you're not the only one who will be getting their father back."

Tobin nodded and left with David, the two of them walked the hall to the port with Jessy following them. Tobin said to David "I would have never seen myself trying to build up courage to do something like this. What would Trill mean by getting her dad back?"

David surprised "Oh that's why she is taking the risk. You see if we save Centauri Nine the professor won't kill her father or at least in theory."

Tobin gave a brief smile "I did even think about that. I guess we all are getting something out of this. You know I don't even know what to do with a blaster?"

David chuckled at Tobin's remark "It's easy, you have a sharp eye. I don't think we are going to have to use it. Here we are and there's the port. That is a pretty easy path to remember. Shall we go now? Perhaps we could make a game of it. The first one of us that is spotted by a guard has to clean Trill's ship. You better be fast boy, I really don't want to touch that Junker."

Tobin smiled "You really hate that ship? OK it's a bet. We better head out."

Dent young

Chapter 15

Up to Us

Tobin gathered up Jessy and they went back to Trill's ship. They settled into the ship and David put in the coordinates. Tobin was nervous and tense about the plan. Months back he was so stubborn and sure of himself. He thought he still must have it in him. "Now I can do it, I have friends to help me." Tobin told himself. The ship shimmied a bit; David said there was a lot of extra magnetic energy causing it. The magnetic energy was building and that the trip back to Nostalgia would be the same if not more turbulent. The ship entered the storage bay as it was meant to. There was no one to be found when the two of them left the ship. With blasters secured they went to the door and David scouted ahead. As they did Tobin noticed the station was much brighter and cleaner. Then he noticed other things about the station looked different too. Tobin thought they must have changed the station a bit later on. When they arrived to where the port was supposed to be, to their dismay they found a scheduling screen and no sign of a port.

David said in a soft voice "We're in trouble; either Marduc forgot or didn't know about the changes done over time to the station. I have no idea how to find the port now."

Tobin whispered "Is there any way we can send Marduc a message, to ask where it was moved from or to?"

David shook his head in dismay "No there isn't away alas. But wait, we can ask him in person."

Tobin confused "How, are we going back?"

David smiled at Tobin with a spark in his eyes "If they haven't moved the security cell we are going to do a jail break. Dent and Marduc aren't the only ones who know where to find a port or will help us."

Tobin pulled out the computer pad "Let's bring up the map and give it a shot."

David looked at the computer pad and found what should be the location of the cell. David said "Found it let's go."

They were lucky to find some older unused corridors to get to the cell. David peeked around the last bend to see how many cells there was. Only three and one security guard David told Tobin he thought it was best to try and make a diversion. Before Tobin or David could think of one Jessy jumped out of his bag. The little guy then ran up to the guard and grabbed the piece of fruit he was eating and ran off. This caused the guard to take chase after Jessy. David grabbed Tobin before he could go after Jessy.

David stated "Let your pet go for right now, we can get him later. I have the codes to open the cell door."

They found a young Dent and Marduc in the middle cell. The two looked to be Tobin's current age. Marduc had a black eye and Dent appeared to have a fat lip.

David looked at them and said "Those guards must have done a good job working you boys over."

Marduc came to the door and said "Who are you?"

David mused "We are the rescue party."

Dent came over to the door and added "That doesn't answer the question. Who sent you?"

David replied "My name is David and this here is Tobin. Trill is the one who sent us here to stop a big mistake."

Marduc alarmed "How did the Time Watchers Committee know what we were doing."

David started the code entry for unlocking the cell "They know everything, let's get you out of there. We need your help."

Marduc lifted an eyebrow and said "Isn't it the other way around."

David said as he opened the door "Never mind we need to find a com port."

Dent quickly said in a panic "We have to stop the professor."

David argued "That's not why we' are here, stopping the professor will change nothing."

Just then Jessy ran up to Tobin. Tobin grabbed him up into his arms and then seen the guard running right at the four of them.

David yelled "Run."

Tobin yelped out "Where?"

Dent took charge by saying "Quick, follow me."

The four of them ran down the service alleys and catwalks of the station. When they finally lost the guard they found themselves in a storage room. Dent looked at Tobin from head to toe.

Dent thought a moment then said "You two don't work with or for the Time Watchers Committee... Who are you really?"

David shook his head in anger as he replied "Dent you have always been smart and yet stupid at the same time. Trill did send us and no we do not work for the watchers. When and where we come from Trill is an outlaw, and you spend every day of your life wishing you could have saved all those people on the planet down there."

Dent stepped back from David and Tobin "I don't trust you."

Tobin interrupted Dent's circling of him and David "If we don't upload this program a time storm will hurt a lot of people. I need you to understand. Dent you are the first person to teach me about time travel. I look up to you, you are my mentor. Please help us make a difference so that you can be proud of what I have done. You stood by me when I made mistakes, you're my friend and you never gave up on me. Together right now we can make something great happen."

Dent pondered Tobin's words and responded "Am I really that awesome in the future?"

Tobin smiled in an attempt to reassure Dent "Yes."

Marduc interjected a gripe "You really think we'll help you by listening to your sad story?"

David stopped him by saying "Marduc do you always have to come across as a jerk? If you come with us and load the program you will see your own handy work."

Marduc was taken aback "I wrote the program?"

David yelled Marduc "You and Dent are the only ones who know how to save that planet and the station."

Marduc decided to yield "OK we'll do this your way. But if the program is malicious and will hurt anyone or this station I will find a way to shut it down."

David said hurriedly "We should go then we have not the time to waste here. Where is the nearest port?"

Dent racked his brain and answered "There is one in an observatory not far from here."

David nodded "OK."

Dent led the way without being spotted by any guards. The first thing they did when they got into the observatory was lock the doors. David walked up to a side panel and found the port needed.

Marduc walked up to him and said "I need to make sure you're doing this right."

David linked the computer pad and the program uploaded itself. David shot a glare at Marduc and said "You should." much to Marduc chagrin.

The program began to install and brought up a screen for them to view the progress

Dent peered at the screen and then asked David "Where is the energy being diverted to exactly?"

David answered "We are going to slingshot it in an arched path to my ship. This will act as a conductor to disperse the energy."

Dent was aghast "Did you leave someone on your ship to do that? They would die!"

David cleverly said "It's a droid no harm will come to anyone."

Tobin was feeling uneasy was it true Trill was going to die?

Dent looked at David with a passing doubt and then said "I find it hard to believe a droid would be accurate enough to do that. So help me, if I find out you left someone there I will hunt you down and see that you are held accountable for it."

During Dent's speech the station vibrated and hummed. Dent had paused mid rant "What was that?"

David checked his T.I.P. "That would be our equipment arriving. Now we can start running the next step in the program."

The screen showed the processes going perfect. It didn't take long for guards to show up and start pounding and blasting at the door.

Marduc commented as he looked towards the door "The Professor must have caught on to us. It will not take him long to stop the program from running."

David gestured to Tobin to come over to him. When Tobin was near David, he handed a coding device to him. David then said "Start this patch program it has security codes for the door."

Tobin nodded and took it to the door and started entering the codes. Marduc and Dent were getting antsy.

Marduc quizzed David, "How are we to know if all of this will work?"

David spoke in a blunt manner "You're watching the program for yourself. It will do what it is meant to do. The doubt you have is only in yourself. If Tobin and I fail it will not be only our failure but it will be yours as well. This is your second chance not ours."

At this point Tobin wasn't sure who had more to gain was it David, Dent, or himself? The program was three fourths of the way done, when the power started to flicker, then the lights went out and backup power came on. There was a rumble and building roar throughout the station. The power kicked back on in to full capacity with a blinding light filling the room. The ship came back with full power everything looked OK on the screen, it then booted a script page. All the sudden a mass amount of energy surrounded the station and then shot out into space. It finally went from a big light show to a quiet normal station.

Just then the guards managed to open the doors. One of the guards said for them to move away from the panel. David stood up and took out a small device out of his coat. He then said to the guards "I wouldn't go off doing anything to us. This is a time disperser if I activate it your way, you will be finding parts of your self's scattered all through time. I'm sure it will be a while before anyone could find all your parts and put you back together."

Dent screamed "What are you doing?"

The guard spoke over Dent saying to David "You're bluffing, no such thing exists."

David interjected "What does it matter I've done what I came to do. What do you intend to do about it?"

The guard was unfazed, "I'll take you to the professor and then lock the whole lot of you up."

David responded with a grin "I don't think so." He flashed a badge of sorts and the guards put down their weapons. David then said "That's right you and your boss caught the attention of the Intergalactic Security. I have the authority to stop all your unauthorized activities."

The guard lowered his weapon and motioned for his partner to do the same "Yes Sir."

David continued to put a bit of a performance on by saying "Dent and Marduc here are deputies of mine and you will carry out their orders from here out."

The guards agreed to do so. Marduc worried said "What of the planet?"

David replied "Yes let's see."

They all went to the observatory's viewing window to their delight the plasmatic cluster was gone. David and Tobin went to the ports screen and looked over the program and data they received. Everything was as it should be.

David then turned to everyone and said "Congratulations to a job well done."

Dent interrupted David's accolades "What of the

station?"

David replied to Dent's inquiry "That is something I will have to check in person to really know. I suggest you do the same for yourself. Oh since some time lines will be changed do to us helping you and I heard you at a point in time lost your T.I.P. Trill gave me this mini holo recorder to give to you. She said you would need it."

David took the recorder out of his pocket and gave it to Dent as per Trill's orders. Dent then said "It would be a bit of a cheat to listen to it to be honest. But alas, I don't have much of an option. I need all of what has happened cleared up for me."

David stood next to Tobin and commented to Marduc and Dent "Tobin and I have stayed long enough. Both you Anthony Dent and Marduc need to confront and set the Professor straight. It's up to you two to tie up the loose end. Tobin and I can't help you with this as we have a rendezvous to make."

Marduc interjected as David and Tobin started to take their leave "Well Dent and I have no idea where you came from but I have a feeling we'll be meeting again. I'm not unsure why you really helped us but I do thank you. If you had not helped Dent and I this was sure to have turned this station into space trash."

David replied with a smile and nod "You're welcome."

Tobin took a moment to add "I would only like to see the best happen for the two of you. You both have helped me and I'm happy to do the same for you."

Dent smiled at Tobin as he waved his index finger at him "There is just something about you I like. Enough chat though. Marduc, before the professor thinks he's getting away scot free we had better act."

Marduc agreed and the two of them with the guards were on their way to fulfill justice. This left Tobin and David to make their way back to the time ship.

Tobin asked as they walked "Did Trill make it OK? Will she be OK?"

David answered Tobin as best he could "We won't know until we rendezvous. You did a good job convincing Dent to go along with us."

Tobin shook his head "I only said the truth, do you work for the Intergalactic Security?"

David chuckled as he scratched his beard "Once a long time back I did. I was just happy no one figured my badge has expired. I was thrown out of the force when I helped Dent get out of some trouble?"

Tobin was troubled "And yet he still doesn't trust you."

David let out a sigh "We have always seen things differently."

Tobin had another thought cross his mind "Were you really going to hurt those guards?"

David smirked at Tobin "No, can't go messing up time lines. I was bluffing."

Tobin grinned "You're good at it. Is this the spot we came in?"

David looked around "Looks like it, load up."

Chapter 16

Is Time Travel for Me

The two climbed into the ship and settled themselves in. David set the ship to orbit Alpha Phoenix. When the ship arrived he did scans of the area. Afterwards David brought the ship to when they had last left Nostalgia. He then did another set of scans of the planet and surrounding area. David opened a viewing portal. Tobin could see the planet; it no longer had the pretty gases bubbling and toiling in its atmosphere. Instead he could see it beautiful vast blue oceans and vibrant continents. From the ship Tobin could also see the Gallant and Nostalgia were safe and where they should be.

David announced to Tobin "All the scans read a healthy planet and the stations seem to be fine. We better go to Nostalgia and meet up with the others."

Tobin agreed and in moments the ship was aligned and settled in Nostalgia. Upon leaving the ship to their shock Tobin and David found themselves in the middle of Dent's Shop. Tobin thought it must have been left over residual energy from the storm that caused them to miss the bay. At their arrival Dent didn't seem to know what to say. Dent stood with a look of disbelief.

He then in a loud excited voice said "What are you doing in my old ship? Don't you know this place just went through an extreme time flux caused by the storm? Nothing is working right and it's unstable to travel time here. Oh wait; did you just do what I think you did? The two of you are irresponsible and abused the rules of time travel."

David rather tired from the experience responded "Don't be lecturing us; we were following the instructions you left for Trill to do. I will quote from you that you will once say "Some have to be there to let others do what needs done. Even though I want to fix what has been done I have no other choice but to be a witness to what others can do."

Dent was fuming as he waved his finger in David's face "You put others at risk!"

David pointed a finger back at Dent's face "If the time storm was not stopped both you and I know it would have broken down, destroying and erasing Nostalgia and the Gallant from existence."

Dent lowered his tone "Are you sure the storm is gone?"

Tobin stood silent as David and Dent had their exchange.

David uttered "We just need some final scans."

As the final words of David's sentence came out, the elevator opened and showed Marduc smiling as he hopped out into the shop.

Marduc in a cheerful manner said "Let me wrap things up for you. All scans final and normal as for the Rochelle your parent's ship it is now docking at the

Gallant. And this time stream is not all that altered, at least not by much. Well to say all major events are unaltered."

Dent now calmed some added "That answers that."

Tobin thoughts were filled with a sense emergency asked "What about Trill is she here? Has anyone seen her?"

Marduc looked to Tobin and answered "No sign of her yet. Give her a bit I'm sure she'll get here."

Dent looked to David "About that droid you said you left on your ship..."

Chrissy came up from behind; causing Dent to cut his questioning short. Chrissy demanded everyone's attention and announced "Fauna is on the com system. She wants to talk to you right away."

Dent huffy at being stopped said "Just great timing, as if I need her on my case. We're not finished here, if you all would follow me to my office."

The whole group of them one by one followed Dent down the corridor. Tobin lagged behind fiddling with his bag to check on Jessy. Tobin heard a bit of a rustling behind him. He turned his head to see one of the clothes racks moving. He stopped following the group and went to see what was in the rack. Tobin reached his hand into the rack until he felt what was moving, and then he grabbed and pulled on it. He heard a woman's voice say "Hay." Then an arm came out and pulled him into the rack. In the rack Tobin was delighted to see Trill alive and well.

She shushed him by place a lone finger upon his

lips and said "Be quiet."

Tobin in a whisper said "You're OK, why are you hiding? We did it just like you said."

Trill answered with a mustered smile "It's complicated; I don't want a lecture from Anthony. I have something for you Tobin." Trill handed an electronic card to Tobin. Then she said "It is the master key to my ship. I want you to have it. Trace told me my new one was fixed and all I have to do is go get it. I need you to cover for me so I can go to the bay and get to the ship."

Tobin took the card and replied "OK but where are you going?"

Trill smiled a Tobin "The Pere Cheney ruins on Glavine Five to look for the Sunni crystal."

Tobin with tearful eyes "You will come back to see us?"

Trill looked at Tobin "Yes."

Tobin still doubtful "What do I tell the others?"

Trill winked at Tobin "They did an awesome job. And when I come back it will be epic. Now go before they miss you."

Tobin wiped his eyes "OK."

Tobin came out of the rack and looked around. Luckily the others were in the office still he promptly left to join them. When in the office Tobin stood by the door, to make sure no one could leave and catch Trill off guard.

Dent looked towards Tobin and said "There you are it took a bit but we brought Fauna up on the com and she has something to tell you."

Tobin cleared his voice to say "Yes."

Fauna was up on the com screen and started the conversation with "With great surprise the Rochelle has docked in the Gallant's bay. Your parents are looking for you Tobin. I've tried to do my best to explain their time displacement to them. I don't know entirely what the bunch of you have done to cause this. I have contacted the Time Watchers Committee and nothing done has come up as catastrophic in nature. So let me make this perfectly clear, if you have crossed or bent rules I want to hear no word of it. An odd thing happened as a result of your time play. I got a com message from my husband telling me there had been an application for Tobin accepted by the time watchers committee to train for time travel. Strange things considering you have no ship and my husband who is now alive after being dead for all these years. I thank you for doing this great thing."

Marduc took over by saying "Sure thing you're welcome. So Tobin what are you going to do for a ship?"

Tobin was unsure but answered "I don't know if I want to be a time traveler. I do have this." Tobin showed them the key card Trill gave him.

David grumbled "Great I lost my ship and Tobin is the one who gets a ship given to him."

Dent darted over to Tobin "Let me see that, it's to my old ship. How did you get that?"

Tobin timidly replied "Trill gave me it a little bit ago. She doesn't need it anymore as her new ship is up and running. She's OK and off to get the Sunni Crystal."

Dent befuddled said "I did have that on my

order sheet. She was here and you didn't say a thing. She needs a good scolding for having you cover for her. Tobin I ought to be giving you a stern lecture. In light of everything you still are only eleven and it seems to be easy to persuade you. But you still did a hell of a job one I couldn't do. For that I thank you."

Marduc cut in being a bit of a jerk with "By the way David lied to you about the android."

Dent agitated "I knew it you sent Trill didn't you?"

David defending himself "She insisted on going I did leave the best android there to help her. Marduc you are one to talk you didn't stop her from going either!"

Marduc grinned and replied "There is no stopping her when she makes up her mind."

Dent grunted in disgust "Shame on you both!"

Fauna spoke loudly over the com "At least we know she is OK. Tobin I have done my best to explain about what happen to their ship and your condition to your parents. They understand the terms of it. If Dent thinks its OK I will have you come back to the Gallant. Your parents can help you adjust and become a family once again."

Dent smiled to Tobin and added "I see no reason not to, his parents care can give him more help then I can."

Tobin was delighted and said "I would like that, will I still work for Dent?"

Fauna answered "That would be up to your parents. I will be leaving the station when things settle down, to be with my own family. I have told your parents that you were in an unexplainable accident. They know nothing about you helping in stopping the time storm and your uncle has agreed not to say anything about it to your parents. I trust Anthony can get you back to the Gallant. I don't think there is anything else we need to go over."

Dent seemed pleased overall "I think you've done a good job. We all need to reflect about what has happened. And get back to everyday business we're signing off."

Fauna peered at the group one last time on her monitor "Agreed I'll see Tobin when he gets here. Good tidings until we speak again."

With that said Fauna turned off the communicator. The group of them was quiet just looking at on another.

Then Tobin realized something he then blurted out "Chrissy if the Rochelle is at the Gallant, what are you doing here?"

Chrissy smiled and replied "You are the first to notice, it is a very good question Tobin."

The thought had also struck Dent as he added "I thought it was odd also."

Chrissy composed herself and went on to say "I'll explain, when the storm hit the Rochelle I was working on repairs to one of the thrusters. The storm caused a surge that struck me; I never made it out of the engine area. I only stayed in a living form because of the time storm. Now that it is gone I'm more like a ghost. I still can be seen and felt, but I'm part of time now. I can go anywhere in space and time. Well there are limits to it."

Tobin in a low voice "That is sad, I couldn't help you could I."

Chrissy smiled "Don't be sad for me. I can help you and go on any adventures you need me to."

Dent attempted to lighten the mood "As long as you can still keep my ledger book up to date. Seriously you are welcome to stay here with me."

Marduc was baffled "I thought you would be leaving this old station, when the time storm was gone Anthony."

Dent responded with a confident air about him "I'll be staying here. I want to help time travelers be prepared for the journeys ahead of them. You can say it has become a passion of mine."

Tobin sheepishly said "Chrissy sorry you won't be with your sister."

Chrissy was touched by Tobin's words "Its OK you can help me keep an eye on her."

Tobin smiled as he wiped a tear from his eye "I will. I'll also let her know you love her if I can."

Dent clapped his hands together and commented "OK lots to straighten out starting with the time machine in my shop. Come along Tobin we'll get it parked in one of the bays until you're ready to use it."

David approached Tobin "You know Tobin I am a fully endorsed and sponsored as a time traveler trainer. So if you should ever be in need look me up. I shouldn't be far."

Tobin thought about David's offer "Thanks, but

right now I would like to be with my parents."

Dent remarked to David "I would think you are going to be plenty busy. Setting up a new colony on the planet you fought hard for David. I'm sure Marduc can help you on your way."

Tobin gave Chrissy a big hug and said his good byes to the others. Once in the ship Dent looked at the controls.

It had been so long since being behind the controls. Dent stared blankly and said" It's been some time, oh well it won't be far to park it." Dent engaged the ship and aligned it to settle at the bay. When Dent and Tobin left the ship they found themselves on Alpha Phoenix. The planet was young and untouched ready and waiting for David.

Dent remarked as he rustled his hair "I must be a bit rusty at this. You must say though this is a lovely place?

Tobin responded with a cheerful smile "Even with all the trouble and the not knowing of it all I'm glad we did what we did."

Dent looked at Tobin in admiration and awe "In all my years of trying to undo what the professor did, I would have never thought it was the courage and heart of an eleven year old that would put a stop to the harm and injustice that was caused to so many people. You know some day I wouldn't mind to go on some time travelling adventures. That is if you would go with me."

Tobin was pleased by Dent's statement "I can't think of any better way to spend time with a friend."

Dent gave a pause "You do know that with the

storm being gone I can't cover up the amount of time you're gone from the Gallant anymore. When you are gone for a week your parents will notice that week."

Tobin nodded "Understood taking things slow is fine by me. I already have been cheated out of enough time."

Dent thought perhaps he needed to look the controls over once more "Let's get you back to your parents. I'm sure if we both pilot the ship we can get it back to Nostalgia."

The two of them returned to the ship. Tobin helped put in the coordinates and aligned the ship. Dent initialized the ship and they were back at Nostalgia in a bay. When they came out of the ship Tobin locked down the ship using his key card. In the bay the two had no problem finding a shuttle to get to the Gallant with. It was a normal simple shuttle, Dent decided to let Tobin fly it over to the Gallant. Tobin had caught onto so many things already, that flying the shuttle was posing no problem. Dent had a feeling of pride over Tobin. He wondered how much of their paths would connect. To ponder how much more of Tobin he would see. Before they docked Dent gave a special com link to Tobin. It was small so Tobin could fit it into his pocket. Tobin docked their ship and they were cleared to exit from the shuttle. Fauna was there to greet them personally.

She opened the conversation by saying "Good to see you back safe."

Tobin nodded and Dent replied for him by saying "I'm sure after everything he's been through he's glad to be back."

Fauna was compelled to ask "What did really go

on? You have changed so many things around us for the better."

Dent answered with "I have no idea the one who knows and orchestrated everything was Paz. It appears everyone took cues from her."

Fauna shook her head in slight disbelief "Don't give her that much credit. I have a feeling pieces of the puzzle just happened to have lined up. All she had to do is give it a good shove."

Tobin added his own thoughts "I think it was a lot of dumb luck for us and good ingenuity."

Fauna was satisfied and remarked "I'm happy with that as an answer Tobin. I'll be leaving in a few weeks after I set up a good replacement for my position. I still will be watching over you two though. After all someone needs to keep the both of you out of trouble."

Dent amused commented "You plan on having a nursemaid for us?"

Fauna gave Dent a dumbfounded look. Dent flashed a smirk at Fauna the turned to Tobin and said "Tobin it has been nice having you work for me. I hope to have you back working for me when you are available to do so. As for you Fauna I wish you the best of luck."

Dent patted Tobin's head and smiled knowing they would see each other again. The last thing he said before he left was "I'll be on my way."

Fauna and Tobin watched Dent's shuttle leave. Fauna turned to Tobin and said "Your parents are waiting for you in the lounge. Another thing before I go you need to let me know if you're going to enroll in the time traveling training. You already have what it takes you just need a little maturing."

Tobin pondered a moment and then answered "It would be nice but I need to see how things with my parents go to really know what I need to do."

Fauna motioned for Tobin to lead the way "I'll walk with you as I'm still not sure what they will do."

When they got to the lounge Stan was there, Chrissy's sister and Tobin's parents. When Tobin and Fauna entered the room Tobin's parents looked him over and then rushed to embrace him. Tobin and his family were tearing up with joy to be reunited. Fauna was pleased to see them happy, but knew she would be spending a good part of the week looking after them nonetheless.

His parents were not quite the way Tobin had remembered them. His mother was beautiful and kind but his father seemed to come across as a bumbler. All Tobin's courage seemed to come from his mother. Tobin thought there must have been something changed about them when he went back into time. The next week was fairly uncomfortable for Tobin. He tried to stay with his parent's in their new quarters, but Jessy would not settle down when it came to bed time. Tobin found himself sleeping back in his uncle's quarters as a result. Jessy did not like the new adjustments and it was hard on Tobin too. He had no idea what to think about this new arrangement. Trying to get along with his parents was like living with total strangers.

Tobin told himself he was going to stick it out. But truth be told it was getting to him; his parents would go from treating him as an adult do to his appearance, too bossing him around as a child he still was. Tobin was truly trying to get to know them better. He also found on? You have changed so many things around us for the better."

Dent answered with "I have no idea the one who knows and orchestrated everything was Paz. It appears everyone took cues from her."

Fauna shook her head in slight disbelief "Don't give her that much credit. I have a feeling pieces of the puzzle just happened to have lined up. All she had to do is give it a good shove."

Tobin added his own thoughts "I think it was a lot of dumb luck for us and good ingenuity."

Fauna was satisfied and remarked "I'm happy with that as an answer Tobin. I'll be leaving in a few weeks after I set up a good replacement for my position. I still will be watching over you two though. After all someone needs to keep the both of you out of trouble."

Dent amused commented "You plan on having a nursemaid for us?"

Fauna gave Dent a dumbfounded look. Dent flashed a smirk at Fauna the turned to Tobin and said "Tobin it has been nice having you work for me. I hope to have you back working for me when you are available to do so. As for you Fauna I wish you the best of luck."

Dent patted Tobin's head and smiled knowing they would see each other again. The last thing he said before he left was "I'll be on my way."

Fauna and Tobin watched Dent's shuttle leave. Fauna turned to Tobin and said "Your parents are waiting for you in the lounge. Another thing before I go you need to let me know if you're going to enroll in the time traveling training. You already have what it takes you just need a little maturing."

Tobin pondered a moment and then answered "It would be nice but I need to see how things with my parents go to really know what I need to do."

Fauna motioned for Tobin to lead the way "I'll walk with you as I'm still not sure what they will do."

When they got to the lounge Stan was there, Chrissy's sister and Tobin's parents. When Tobin and Fauna entered the room Tobin's parents looked him over and then rushed to embrace him. Tobin and his family were tearing up with joy to be reunited. Fauna was pleased to see them happy, but knew she would be spending a good part of the week looking after them nonetheless.

His parents were not quite the way Tobin had remembered them. His mother was beautiful and kind but his father seemed to come across as a bumbler. All Tobin's courage seemed to come from his mother. Tobin thought there must have been something changed about them when he went back into time. The next week was fairly uncomfortable for Tobin. He tried to stay with his parent's in their new quarters, but Jessy would not settle down when it came to bed time. Tobin found himself sleeping back in his uncle's quarters as a result. Jessy did not like the new adjustments and it was hard on Tobin too. He had no idea what to think about this new arrangement. Trying to get along with his parents was like living with total strangers.

Tobin told himself he was going to stick it out. But truth be told it was getting to him; his parents would go from treating him as an adult do to his appearance, too bossing him around as a child he still was. Tobin was truly trying to get to know them better. He also found himself not agreeing with their opinions on most things. His parents were of the idea that he should become an ecologist and went on to dictate what he was to do with his life. When Tobin suggested that perhaps he could go and setup colonies or stations with his parent they would have none of it. They wanted him to stay in a safe environment. This bothered Tobin, his parents lacked concern for themselves and it was hard to get them to listen to what he wanted to do.

Tobin found himself reflecting about everything that had transpired in one of the viewing rooms, so he could see Alpha Phoenix as his mind wandered. He let Jessy play in the room; the little guy was too restless in his bag. As Tobin was thinking he noticed one of the youths was playing with Jessy. Tobin gave him a smile and then the youngster stopped playing and came up to Tobin.

The youth asked "Where is the little boy who has this pet? I haven't seen him for a long time and yet you have his pet."

Tobin stood silent for a moment then improvised by saying "The boy left the pet with me because his family came back to get him. They all left to live on a colony planet together."

Not really a lie to the youth Tobin thought. It was at one time one of Tobin's fantasies and his parents had come back.

The youth then said "I wish he left his pet with me. Can I play with him for a while more?"

Tobin smiled and said "Yes." Tobin stood and watched them play until the youth's mother came and took him away.

Tobin enjoyed seeing the delight in the youth's eyes, yet Tobin himself was torn. He had the trusting and hope of a youth, yet he could comprehend the knowledge and responsibility of an adult. He knew this was not the place for him anymore. Tobin made up his mind to go and talk to Fauna. He figured he could become a time traveler and work for Dent finding him items for his store. Maybe through his journey he could find out why things didn't feel right.

The End

Trace

About the Author

I started the story A time in Nostalgia during a time of my life that I was losing every thing important to me. It was a time I had to work hard to get through. Writing this story came as comfort and a focus point for me. I hope to bring a story that is close to me to others to enjoy.

I attended Baker College of Cadillac and obtained a Degree in Graphics design. I have lived in Northern Michigan for most of my life and am happily married to Craig Garrow co-writer of our book.

Made in the USA
Charleston, SC
17 February 2016